**"Some women think I'm pretty handsome,"
Jason said with a definite growl in his voice.**

"I'm sure some do," Riki said in a voice that was pure sugar. "But don't you think a seven-year-old is a little young to have her head turned by a pretty face?"

"Some women like their men rich." The growling was growing louder.

"I guess buying ice cream for the whole ball team can be counted as rich to some. But pretty soon Charlie will learn that money isn't everything," Riki said innocently.

"Some women like their men experienced."

"In what?"

"In knowing how to make a woman's body come alive during lovemaking."

Riki's mouth went dry. Her whole body was coming alive, and he wasn't even touching her.

"And what do you like in your men, Riki?" The growling had stopped, but there was a definite roar now.

She said the first thing that came into her mind. "Roller coaster rides." Then Jason's mouth covered hers. . . .

WHAT ARE *LOVESWEPT* ROMANCES?

They are stories of true romance and touching emotion. We believe those two very important ingredients are constants in our highly sensual and very believable stories in the *LOVESWEPT* line. Our goal is to give you, the reader, stories of consistently high quality that may sometimes make you laugh, sometimes make you cry, but are always fresh and creative and contain many delightful surprises within their pages.

Most romance fans read an enormous number of books. Those they truly love, they keep. Others may be traded with friends and soon forgotten. We hope that each *LOVESWEPT* romance will be a treasure—a "keeper." We will always try to publish

LOVE STORIES YOU'LL NEVER FORGET
BY AUTHORS YOU'LL ALWAYS REMEMBER

The Editors

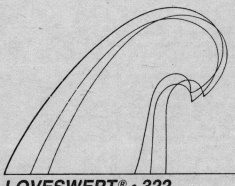

LOVESWEPT® • 322

Marcia Evanick
Perfect Morning

 BANTAM BOOKS
TORONTO • NEW YORK • LONDON • SYDNEY • AUCKLAND

PERFECT MORNING
A Bantam Book / April 1989

If you would be interested in receiving protective vinyl
covers for your Loveswept books, please write to this address
for information:

Loveswept
Bantam Books
P.O. Box 985
Hicksville, NY 11802

ISBN 0-553-21997-9

Published simultaneously in the United States and Canada

PRINTED IN THE UNITED STATES OF AMERICA

O   0 9 8 7 6 5 4 3 2 1

*To my husband, Michael,
who's my conscience, my heart,
and my life.*

One

Chickens! There must have been ten chickens and two geese running around in circles, squawking and clucking. More than the birds, though, the kids held Jason Nesbit's attention. Seven of them were trying to catch the chickens; each was slipping and sliding and covered from head to toe in mud. It was a total free-for-all. Laughter and screams filled the air.

Every time the kids made a circle around the chickens, the chickens charged and the kids ended up in the mud as they tried to grab them. No one seemed to mind the mud. Everyone was having a ball. Jason couldn't tell which were boys and which were girls, except the oldest.

Even with all that mud, he couldn't mistake the generous fullness of her breasts or the enticing curve of her hips. He grinned as she landed on her well-shaped fanny once again. One of the little ones toddled over and calmly scooped up a handful of mud and dropped it down her back. He could hear the shrieks from where he stood, then he heard her laughter. The happy sound seemed to cascade over him, and he couldn't tear his gaze from her. Then he pulled himself up short. He wasn't there to ogle a young woman whom he presumed was Mrs. McCormick's babysitter. He was there to find his daughter.

And where was she? He studied the boisterous children, but knew his daughter wasn't among them. He'd been told Charleen had been traumatized by the accident that had killed her mother and stepfather. She wouldn't be playing in the mud.

So where was she?

The babysitter was now crawling around on her hands and knees, pretending to be a mud monster and chasing the smallest children. One of the other kids jumped on her back, yelling "Giddy-up!" She bucked him off and pawed the air. Another kid jumped on to try his luck, but he met with the same result.

She trotted away from the children, over to a girl Jason hadn't noticed before. She was small, perhaps only four years old, and her arms wrapped around the neck of the biggest Great Dane he had ever seen. Dressed in jeans, T-shirt, and sneakers, she was the only clean child there. Could this be . . . ?

The babysitter spoke to the girl and held out her arms. The girl shook her head and tightened her grip on the dog, then gazed across the backyard at Jason.

Lightning shot through him when he saw her eyes. His eyes. She had his silver eyes. Oh, God, this was his daughter. Charleen. Impulsively, he started forward.

Riki McCormick noticed Charlie staring at something, then caught movement out of the corner of her eye. A man was walking toward her, around the corner of the back porch. Oh, no, she thought. It couldn't be. She shaded her eyes to get a better look and frowned. It would be him. With all the rotten luck, why now? She glanced down at the mud caked on her body. Her band of Munchkins looked just as bad. There was nowhere to hide. There wasn't a rock big enough for her to crawl under, let alone with six children. Chin up, old girl, she told herself. What was the worst he could do? Take Charlie, and he was going to do that anyway.

There was no mistake, she thought. That had to be Jason Nesbit, Charlie's father. The resemblance was astonishing. He had stopped walking when he saw her watching him, and she took a moment to study him. She judged him to be about six feet tall. He was wearing black trousers and a white short-sleeved shirt. In the shade of the porch his hair looked black, and it was a bit longer than a typical businessman's. She wasn't positive, but she'd bet he had the same silver eyes as his daughter. The major difference between the two was Jason Nesbit had a smile playing across his face and Charlie never smiled. With a glance at the girl, Riki gave a loud, high-pitched whistle that quieted everyone immediately. All seven children faced her and waited.

"Kids, I believe we have company. Up to the porch, everybody. Travis, please help Jake." Riki reached down for Billy-Jo's hand and they slowly made their way to the back porch.

Jason was amazed. He hadn't seen obedience

like that since his days in the Marines. She was some babysitter.

The young woman stopped in front of him. "Hello, you must be Jason Nesbit." She stuck her hand out for a shake, glanced at it, and withdrew it. "Sorry about that. I'll wait until I've washed up a bit."

"Yes, I'm Jason," he said, "but you and the gang have me at a disadvantage."

"I talked to you on the phone several times. I'm Erika McCormick, Riki to my friends."

"You're Mrs. McCormick?" Jason tried, but he couldn't hide the surprise. At her stiffening, he quickly added, "I mean, you look so . . . uh, young." He accompanied this statement with his most winning smile.

Riki's heart stopped. Her stomach dropped to her knees, flipped over three times, and died. Her mouth went totally dry, and she slowly ran her tongue over her lips. She couldn't help noticing that Jason Nesbit was following every movement. She also couldn't help noticing the fire burning in his eyes, and said the first thing that came into her mind. "You're early."

As Jason stared at her small pink tongue, his mind turned over a dozen different possible uses for it. When it slipped back in between her soft lips, his gaze traveled downward, past a long neck that was streaked with dirt to a mud-soaked T-shirt clinging to a pair of tantalizing breasts. As a streak of desire shot across his abdomen he silently cursed his overactive hormones. For cripesake, he was here to meet his daughter. He was still amazed that he had been a father for the past six years and never knew it.

He pulled his thoughts back to the conversation. "Sorry about being early. I took an earlier flight than planned and there wasn't any time to notify you."

Riki felt a tug on her hand. She looked down at Billy-Jo as if she couldn't for the life of her figure out how she got there. "Oh, I'm sorry, honey. It wasn't nice of Mommy not to introduce you." She turned back to Jason with a smile and a small shrug, as if to say "here goes."

"Kids, I want you all to meet Mr. Jason Nesbit. He is going to become a very close friend of the family. Mr. Nesbit will be spending a lot of time with us for the next couple of weeks. I want you all to behave and treat him like family." Her glance pinned her oldest sons, identical twins, and they flushed a bright red. "Right, boys?"

There was a chorus of "Yes, Mom." She nodded and glanced at Jason. "Don't be embarrassed if you forget a name or two. It's a lot to handle all at once. The twins are Travis and Trevor. It's quite impossible to tell them apart at times. They are six going on eighteen, and they have been known to strike terror into the hearts of the good citizens of Mountain View. Don't let the angelic looks fool you for a minute, or you're a goner."

She rested her hand on the head of a boy with blonde hair. "This is Jake. As you probably haven't noticed, Jake is blind. Most people don't notice it at first. He's been blind since birth. Please don't feel sorry for him. Believe me, he makes it up in other areas. He can hear a whisper a mile away. Right, son?"

"Yes, ma'am." The smile on Jake's face showed how proud he was of that.

"Nice meeting you, Jake," Jason said.

"Pete over there is the oldest of the tribe. As you can see, he wears a hearing aid. Lord, Pete, I hope you didn't get any mud in it this time."

"No, ma'am, it's just fine. Nice meeting you, Mr. Nesbit."

"My pleasure, Pete. You were pretty fast trying to catch those chickens."

Pete's face turned pink from the compliment as he smiled.

Riki glanced at the next in line, shook her head, and flashed a look skyward as if asking for help. "This is Andrew. He just turned four and has more curiosity in his little finger than every soul in the town of Mountain View put together. If you are ever alone with him, please beware. He will ask you anything at anytime. Believe me, it is usually at the worst possible time too."

"Hello, Andrew. It's a pleasure to meet you."

"Are you going to be my daddy?"

Riki choked and went white. She didn't have the guts to look at Jason, so she stared daggers at Andrew.

After recovering from his shock, Jason chuckled. "I don't think so, Andrew. I don't think Mrs. McCormick's husband would approve." There, that ought to satisfy him, he thought smugly.

"Mom doesn't have a husband," Andrew said. "Just us kids."

Riki thought she might kill him. She was just deciding which method. Boiling oil, swords at dawn? No, she'd run him over with his Tonka truck, a simple accident. She'd collect the insurance money and go to Tahiti.

"No husband?" Jason asked, staring at her. No husband and all these kids?

"I'm a widow." He didn't comment, and she added, "I warned you about Andrew. You're on your own now.

"This little darlin' is Billy-Jo, my youngest. She's two and is just learning to go potty, so be prepared to clap a lot. She insists everyone must clap. Right, darlin'?"

Jason bent to Billy-Jo's level and smiled. "It's nice to meet you, Billy-Jo. You're as pretty as your mother." He ruffled her mud-caked hair as he straightened.

Riki looked behind her at the lone figure and the dog. Swallowing hard, she said, "Charlie, please come here for a minute."

Jason's heart stopped as the little girl tightened her hold on the dog, but hesitantly stepped forward. She halted a few feet away from him, and he squatted down to get a better look at her.

If his ex-wife, Cynthia, hadn't been killed in the auto accident over six months ago, he'd be tempted to wring her neck. On the other hand, if she and her current husband hadn't died, he would never have known about his daughter. His first reaction upon receiving the summons from the Child Welfare Department a week ago had been arrogance, but curiosity had gotten the better of him. When the social worker told him about Charleen, he'd expressed his doubts about the parentage, despite his name being on her birth certificate. After he'd seen her picture, all doubts were erased. She was the spitting image of him, except with longer hair and frightened eyes.

While he had sat there staring at her picture, the social worker had explained Charleen's problem. Since she had learned of her mother's and, as far as she knew, her father's deaths, she hadn't spoken one word.

Immediately after the accident, Charleen had been placed in a foster home in Richmond, Virginia. She had become more withdrawn, though, and had then been sent to a Mrs. Erika McCormick in Mountain View, Virginia.

The social worker assured Jason that Mrs. McCormick was well qualified in rearing foster children with special problems, and had already achieved some positive results with Charleen. After several conversations with the Child Welfare Department and Mrs. McCormick, Jason had agreed to go to Mountain View and get to know his daughter before attempting to take her back to Texas with him.

After a hectic week of tying up loose ends and turning his construction business over to his brother-in-law, Sam, Jason had hopped the first available plane to Virginia.

"Jason," Riki said, "I would like you to meet Charleen. She turned six in March. She doesn't talk much right now, but one day she will."

Riki's voice cracked. She couldn't help it. Jason's expression was one of hope and eager anticipation, but he couldn't express what he was feeling. It might set Charlie back. All the past few months' progress would be for nothing.

Jason's arms ached from not moving. All he wanted was to hold his daughter. The fear was back in her eyes—his eyes—and he had put it there. He knew he had to go slowly, but it hurt. God, did it hurt. He turned to Riki for help.

She read the appeal in his eyes. "Charlie, why don't you show Mr. Nesbit Tiny?"

Charlie glanced from Riki to Jason, then pushed the Great Dane forward.

"Mr. Nesbit," Riki said, "meet Tiny. Tiny follows Charlie everywhere. They have become quite inseparable these last few months. Tiny even sleeps at the foot of Charlie's bed. Right, Charlie?"

Charlie scratched behind the dog's ear, looked once more at Jason, and shyly slid to the back of the pack.

"Okay," Riki said, trying to make light of the emotional moment, "now that you have met the whole bunch, do you want to run?"

"Who, me?" Jason asked innocently.

"If you had any sense you would."

"Doesn't say much for you."

"Who, me?" At his raised eyebrows, she gasped and stared at him in mock horror. "Oh my lord, you'll guess my mission on this planet if I'm not careful."

"What's your mission?" he whispered, after glancing around to make sure he wasn't overheard.

"They sent me down here to figure out why earthlings have children when they're aggravating, overbearing, and demanding." She wiggled her eyebrows like Groucho Marx.

He couldn't help but go along with the joke. "Did you figure it out yet?"

"Of course. Don't I look like a higher form of intelligent life?" She stared down her nose at him, never giving it a thought that she was covered in mud from head to toe.

He grinned, wishing he could get a good look at her. The only thing he knew for sure was her eyes were emerald green. "What's the secret?"

"The sex is great." After delivering that bomb,

she said, "Fall in troops. Baths for everyone, except Charlie. Charlie, would you mind keeping Mr. Nesbit company in the front parlor while the rest of us get cleaned up?"

Jason was stunned. He would never have expected a reply like that. He was still staring after her and the kids when he noticed Charlie and Tiny waiting patiently for him. He gave himself a shake, smiled at Charlie, and followed her inside.

The inside of the house was gorgeous, belying the fact that the outside was falling down. He guessed the interior was being restored to its original state. Not all the work was done, and he guessed that could take years. The house was clean though cluttered, with toys and books lying around. There wasn't any dirt, but you could tell children lived and played there.

Jason followed Charlie and Tiny into the front parlor. Most of the room was done, except the fireplace. He sat on the Victorian love seat. Charlie, after dusting off the seat of her pants, sat in a wing chair with Tiny curled up at her feet. Jason glanced at the dog and wondered about the relationship. Would he have to take the dog back to Texas too? It looked that way. He guessed it was Riki's dog, and hoped she would sell it. But was it safe for Charlie to cling to the Great Dane? It had to outweigh her by ninety pounds at least. Who had named it Tiny, for cripesake?

Riki probably. He never liked girls being called by a boy's name. It always seemed masculine. Now he had a daughter going by the name of Charlie, being raised by a woman named Riki. Yet there was no way that Riki was masculine. He'd had a very good look at her derriere as she marched the troops in. No, she certainly wasn't masculine.

Once more, Jason had to drag his wandering thoughts away from Riki. He glanced at Charlie and started to get nervous. He didn't know where to begin with his own daughter. He read her T-shirt and asked, "I see you're the bat boy. Do you like it?"

Charlie simply stared at him, and he decided there was something weird about having your own eyes gaze at you. He took a deep breath. "Does Tiny always follow you around?" He caught the faintest glimmer of laughter in her eyes before she looked down at Tiny. When she returned her gaze to his, the emotion was gone. Her eyes were empty as before. Jason was trying to figure out why she was covering up her emotions when the noise of children banging down the stairs caught his attention.

One of the twins came running into the room at full speed with the other right on his heels, screaming, "Give me back my shirt."

"It's mine, you nerd."

"Is not."

"Is too."

Jason wondered if he should intervene before they came to blows. He didn't notice Pete and Jake enter the room.

"Dammit," Pete said, "are you guys shouting or is this thing on the blink again?" He tapped the box he kept in his shirt pocket.

"They are shouting, as usual," Jake said. "You better not let Mom hear you cuss like that. You remember what happened the last time." He chuckled.

"Mom, Mom, Pete's cussing again." Andrew, who had slipped into the room unnoticed, started clapping his hands, a gleeful expression on his face.

"Give me my shirt."

"It isn't yours."

"Is too."

"Damn box."

"Mom, Mom, he cussed again."

"Shut up, Andrew."

Jason stared at the boys, wondering what he should do in this madhouse. He glanced at Charlie to see her reaction. He wasn't totally positive, but he believed a smile was beginning to form at the corners of her mouth. He was still looking at her when a naked body flew by.

"Billy-Jo," Riki called from upstairs, "get back here. You are going to catch pneumonia."

"Potty, potty," Billy-Jo said, beaming.

"Does that mean she has to go?" Jason asked. He knew absolutely nothing about potty training.

"Naw," Travis or Trevor said. "It means we all have to clap."

Everyone except Charlie began clapping. Billy-Jo walked over to Charlie, stuck a thumb in her mouth, and waited. After a moment, Charlie patted her on top of her head and clapped.

It was the first time Jason had seen her show any emotion, and his heart seemed to clench. How long would it take her to show some emotion toward him?

Riki entered the room carrying clothes. "Billy-Jo, you are going to have to curb this desire to walk around the house naked within the next couple of years."

She proceeded to dress Billy-Jo, and Jason couldn't help staring at her. This was the mud ball from the back porch? If it weren't for her voice and the emerald eyes, he wouldn't believe it.

She was the most adorable package of woman-hood he had ever seen squeezed into jeans and a polo shirt. She wasn't a classic beauty. She wasn't tall and skinny. She was perfect. If she was five four she was lucky, and she wasn't the least bit plump. She was a woman, soft and cuddly, her curves just where they should be, especially her derriere. Jason had always had a soft spot for that part of a woman's anatomy. And if he kept watching, it wouldn't be soft for long.

He shifted his gaze to safer territory. Her auburn hair tumbled below her shoulders, and the sun pouring in the window highlighted the red. She had a healthy complexion, the kind that said she spent a lot of time outdoors. His glance slid to her mouth—perfect, sensual, exciting, kissable.

Riki glanced up and smiled. Jason felt his heart skip two beats, then it started in on double time.

"Mom," Andrew said, "Pete was saying curses again."

"Andrew, what have I told you about tattling?" Riki frowned at her son, then glanced at Pete. "Do you want to be punished again?"

"No, ma'am."

"Then you better not let me hear that kind of language again." She stood up. "Okay, gang. I want all the dirty clothes out by the washer. You can go out to play, but this time keep out of the mud. Andrew, you stay in the yard. Billy-Jo, you can help Mommy with dinner. Mr. Nesbit, would you like to join me for a cup of coffee?"

"Okay, and the name's Jason."

"Only if you call me Riki."

She led the way into a huge kitchen that had just about every modern convenience. There was a dishwasher, a microwave, and an assortment of small appliances that Jason didn't recognize. A large pine picnic table sat in the middle of the room, with benches on either side and a chair at each end. Jason sat on one of the benches. Billy-Jo climbed up next to him and stuck her thumb in her mouth.

"Here, Mom," Travis, or was that Trevor, said as he laid muddy jeans on top of the washer. The rest of the gang filed in and deposited their dirty clothes.

"Cookies are on the counter," Riki said, "but only take two. Dinner won't be that much longer."

Jason noticed that not one of the kids took more than two cookies. When Charlie entered the room with Tiny, she took two cookies as well. She put one in her mouth and fed the other to Tiny.

Riki chuckled. "He's going to get as fat as an elephant if you keep feeding him cookies, Charlie."

Charlie glanced up at Riki. Jason guessed that was her way of showing she had heard and understood. He watched as she turned and left with Tiny.

Riki was measuring coffee into the drip coffee brewer when Billy-Jo said, "Cook, cook."

"In a minute, darlin'. Let Mommy finish here first."

"Would you like me to get them for you?" Jason asked. At Billy-Jo's nod he got two cookies for her and handed them to her.

"You just made a friend for life," Riki said as she set a cup of milk in front of Billy-Jo.

"I wish they were all that easy," he muttered.

"I know it must be hard on you, but I believe this is the best way." Riki smiled, trying to ease the strain.

"Okay, you're the boss. What now?"

She handed him his coffee, then sat down across from him. "First, dinner. You are joining us, of course. The couple who live next door went away a few days ago. They've gone to stay with their daughter, who is going to have a baby any day now. They'll be gone for two weeks or so. Anyway, I usually watch their house for them whenever they're away. I explained the situation here and they agreed to allow you to sleep in their guest room while you're here. You can join us for breakfast, lunch, and dinner. You can virtually live here, except you have to sleep there."

"Why?"

"Why what?"

"Why do I have to sleep over there?"

Riki didn't like that gleam in his eyes. "Because it wouldn't be proper for you to sleep here."

"Why? Do you attack strange men in the middle of the night?" Jason couldn't help himself. She was actually blushing. He hadn't seen a girl blush since high school.

"Of course not!" Riki was more angry at herself for getting flustered than at Jason for teasing her. *He must think you're a real country bumpkin,* she told herself, *blushing and stumbling over your own tongue.* "Look, Jason, I'm in the process of trying to adopt Jake and Pete, and something I don't need is gossip."

"Why not Charlie or the others?"

"I always knew Charlie had a father somewhere. Even though it took so long to find you, I never got my hopes up. If you were dead and there was no family, I would have applied to adopt her too. As for the others, I don't have to adopt them."

"Thanks for wishing me dead, and why don't you have to adopt the others?"

"They're mine."

He raised his brows. "All of them?"

She stiffened her shoulders. "There are only four."

"Whoa, Mama Bear, I have nothing against four kids. It's just that you don't look like you had four."

"Right now I'm the mother of seven. Any complaints?"

"Not a one. I didn't mean to imply that you weren't a good mother or anything. It's just that you don't look like my idea of a mother of seven." He leered comically at her and proceeded to check out her body.

Riki could feel the blush starting at her neck. She quickly put her coffee cup down and stood. "Let's go next door, and I'll show you around." Grabbing Billy-Jo's hand, she headed for the back door.

Two

Lying in his bed that night and staring up at the ceiling, Jason couldn't quell his excitement. Damn, if this day hadn't turned out totally different from what he had expected. He smiled when he thought about dinner. He had never sat down at a table with seven children before. It was total chaos, but the feeling of love was ever present.

After Riki had shown him the Stanleys' place, the boys had helped him carry in his few pieces of luggage. He had then joined Charlie on the back porch. She hadn't seemed to mind that he was there, but she hadn't acknowledged him either. When Riki called everyone in for dinner, they had both gone inside. He had carried in the meat loaf and mashed potatoes. Riki had carried in the rest, and they had all sat down.

Jason was on his second mouthful, after complimenting Riki on the best meat loaf he had ever tasted, when all hell broke lose.

"Mom, Travis kicked me."

"Did not."

"Travis, please stop it."

"Stop what?"

"Not you, Pete. Please turn up your hearing aid."

"Mom, Andrew stuck his fingers in my mashed potatoes."

"Riki, why is Billy-Jo plastering mashed potatoes on her hair?"

"Billy-Jo, darlin', stop that."

"Who took my fork?"

"Boys, give Jake back his fork. It isn't nice to tease him."

"But, Mom . . ."

"No, buts."

"He broke the dam in my mashed potatoes and got gravy in my peas."

"Jake?"

"I was trying to find my napkin."

"Two places down?"

"Riki! Billy-Jo is choking!"

"No, she's not, Jason. It's her way of saying she's done."

"Why is she blue?"

"Good acting."

Jason stole a glance at Charlie. She was busy eating, apparently not paying one bit of attention. But he saw a smile trying to break free. So she did understand what was going on, he thought. She just wasn't a part of it—yet.

After everyone helped clear the table, they all gathered in the front parlor. Since it wasn't a school night, the kids didn't have to do homework. Riki ended up on the floor with Travis, Trevor, Jake, and Pete, reading the continuing story of Robinson Crusoe. Andrew climbed up on the couch and handed Jason a storybook about life on a farm. Jason had never read a child a story before, but with an encouraging smile from Riki he gave it a shot. Charlie sat on the sidelines listening to everything while slowly running her fingers up and down Tiny's spine.

Jason had no idea where the time went, but the next thing he knew Riki was telling everyone too get ready for bed. He ruffled Billy-Jo's hair and stood her on the floor. She had managed to climb up on his lap as he was reading to Andrew. He had liked holding her, smelling the scent of baby shampoo and watching her suck her thumb. He had pointed out all the animals in the book to see if Andrew or Billy-Jo knew their names.

As the boys climbed the steps, either Travis or Trevor, he wasn't sure which, asked if he wanted to see their baseball card collection. He glanced at Riki. She nodded, and he followed the crowd.

Upstairs two huge rooms overlooked the front of the house with a door between them. One room was papered in a baseball print with solid blue curtains, while the other was painted blue with baseball print curtains. The room that was painted was the twins' room, and the walls were covered with pennants of all the major baseball teams.

Jason sat down on the bottom bunk bed as Riki took Billy-Jo and Charlie to their room. Travis and Trevor showed him their shoe boxes filled with cards. Pete showed him his shoe box, too, which was more than half filled. He explained he had just started collecting. Andrew showed him a green stuffed animal and told him it was the Philly Phanatic.

Jake stood in front of him, his hands behind his back. "Bet you can't guess what I have."

"More baseball cards?"

"Nope. What would a blind kid do with baseball cards?"

Jason studied Jake, and realized the boy wasn't too bothered about being blind. Jason could imagine the anger a child might have, but Jake didn't seem to be angry at all. He wasn't a bit rebellious. He fit right into this large family, and Jason had trouble remembering he was blind.

"I give up," he said. "What is it?"

Jake brought his hand from behind his back. He was holding a baseball autographed by ten members of the Philadelphia Phillies.

"Hey, this is great," Jason said. "Where did you get it?"

"Uncle Frank," one of the twins said. "He's Mom's brother. He lives up there near the Phillies, but he travels all the time. He's the one who sends us all this neat stuff. When he sent the baseball, we took a vote and decided since Jake couldn't see the baseball cards we'd give him the ball. At least he can hold that. Right?"

Jason had to swallow hard and clear his throat. Damn, he thought. The boys really loved one another. "I think you guys made the right decision."

Billy-Jo, dressed in her pajamas, came flying into the room and jumped up on the bed next to Jason. Charlie entered the room, too, and stood in the corner with the ever-present Tiny at her side. Riki came in last, glanced around, and gave the boys a stern look.

"Okay, guys, I asked you to get ready for bed. Let's move it."

As the boys scrambled for their pajamas, Riki eyed Jason sitting on the bed with Billy-Jo curled up at his side. Damn if he didn't just fit right in, she thought. He looked like he belonged to this crazy family.

Those are dangerous thoughts there, girl, she told herself. Jason was Charlie's father. He lived in Texas and most importantly, he would be leaving soon.

"Charlie," she said, "why don't you and Billy-Jo show Jason your room? You can show him Dust Ball too. Just be careful she doesn't bite him."

Jason followed Charlie and Tiny out of the room, holding Billy-Jo's hand. As he passed Riki he raised an eyebrow. "Dust Ball?"

"You'll see." She smiled her most innocent smile.

He followed Charlie to a room overlooking the back and side yards. It was pink and decorated with a popular doll character. There were two single beds, one with a juvenile guardrail up on one side. He gathered that was Billy-Jo's bed.

Charlie walked over to a twenty-gallon fish tank that sat on a table in the corner. She put her hand in and gently lifted out a guinea pig. As she stroked the animal, she sat on her bed. Jason squatted in front of her. He was staring at her hands, so small and gentle. He raised his gaze and stared into eyes so much like his own.

"So, this must be Dust Ball." Charlie nodded once. He slowly lifted his arm. "May I pet her?" She tightened her grip on Dust Ball and violently shook her head. "Okay, I won't pet her. I wouldn't hurt her, just like I wouldn't hurt you."

Charlie glanced down at the guinea pig, then back up at Jason, still shaking her head.

"Bite, bite," Billy-Jo said. She was pulling at his hand, backing away from Dust Ball.

"Oh, I see," he said. "You're trying to tell me she'll bite me if I pet her." Charlie nodded. "Well then, thank you for warning me. I don't want to be bitten by her." He sat there smiling at Charlie until Billy-Jo handed him a doll that was half her size.

"Mine."

"She's very pretty, Billy-Jo, just like you. And she's big. Where did you get her?"

"Cole Crank."

"Cole Crank?"

"She's telling you Uncle Frank," Travis—or was it Trevor?—said. He was leaning against the door jamb. "She can't talk right. But Mom says not to worry. She said pretty soon we would all be praying to our Maker that she would be quiet. Mom said you can come and say good night to us now. And she said you'll be here tomorrow. After church can you take us down to the baseball field and help us practice? Mom's okay, but she is only a girl."

Jason was still chuckling when he entered the boys' room. Riki was bending over Andrew, tucking in his covers. She placed a kiss on his forehead. "Try to stay in bed tonight."

"Oh, Mom." He glanced behind her to Jason. " 'Night, Jason. See you in the morning."

" 'Night, Andrew." He reached past Riki to ruffle his hair.

Jake and Pete's bunk bed was on the other side of the room. Jason walked over to them and ruffled Jake's hair too. "Good night, Jake. I'll see you in the morning." He looked up into the top bunk.

" 'Night, Pete." When there was no response, he glanced over his shoulder at Riki.

"He can't hear you. He doesn't sleep with his hearing aid." Standing on the lower bunk, she kissed Pete and whispered good night. Jason reached up to pat Pete's shoulder and said good night too. He had no idea whether Pete could hear him or not. He was leaving the room when Pete spoke.

"Good night, Jason. See you in the morning. Are you going to help us with baseball practice?"

He turned back and said "Yes" while nodding his head.

"Good."

He followed Riki into the other bedroom. She leaned over the boy in the bottom bunk, kissed him, and whispered, " 'Night, Travis."

"I'm Trevor."

"Whoever." She stood on the lower bed, kissed the boy in the top bunk, and said, " 'Night, Travis."

"I'm Trevor."

"Whoever."

Jason chuckled as he approached the beds. "Good night, boys, whoever you are." He patted each on the shoulder and followed Riki from the room.

She sighed. "Five down, two to go."

In the girls' bedroom, she tucked the covers tight around Charlie. "Good night, honey. See you in the morning." She kissed her cheek, then patted Tiny, who was lying at the foot of Charlie's bed. " 'Night, mutt. You take care of my girls, you hear."

She walked over to Billy-Jo, who was somewhat lost in such a large bed with about six dolls and twelve stuffed animals in it. She tucked her in and kissed her, brushing the hair out of her eyes. "Now, young lady, I don't want you roaming the house tonight, and I don't want any night visitors either. Got it?" Billy-Jo just smiled. "Good night, baby."

Riki walked to the door, then turned to watch Jason. He seemed lost, not knowing what to do. He was fine with the boys, but he was freezing up with Charlie. As he stood there with his back to her, she noticed the broad shoulders tapering down to a narrow waist and slim hips. Nice, she thought. Real nice. She wondered what he would look like without the shirt. Probably muscular and tan. Hell, she could even picture him in a bathing suit. His thighs would be hard and lean. Some men looked silly in a bathing suit, but she was sure Jason wouldn't. She couldn't imagine him looking silly in anything. And she could imagine him looking fantastic in nothing. Heavens, where had that thought come from? *You really are getting to be a dirty old lady, thinking thoughts like that, she told herself. And about Charlie's father, no less.*

Damn, she thought, why couldn't she be one of those women who could have an affair with a man they knew next to nothing about and calmly walk away? The sex might relieve some of the tensions she was feeling, but she didn't think it would help the ache that was down deep. She wanted to be held tight, have someone help make the decisions, someone she could talk to, lean on. Why had she read that article in that women's magazine about nearing her sexual peak? And why had the good Lord decided to send Jason, the hunk, to her now? She'd finally gotten her life together just the way she wanted it and—bam!

Real cute, God. Are You and Saint Peter up there taking bets on this one, and having a good laugh? She could picture it now, He and Saint Peter laughing, saying, "If seven kids didn't make her crack, we'll send her a tall, dark, and handsome man to live with for a couple of weeks. That will do it."

She shook her head to clear her thoughts and refocused on Jason. He was kissing Billy-Jo good night.

He walked slowly over to Charlie's bed and patted Tiny. Then he looked down at Charlie and gently pushed a lock of her hair back. Riki noticed that his hand was trembling.

"Good night, sweetheart," he whispered, and bent down to kiss her cheek. Riki was surprised Charlie didn't back away. She just stared at Jason.

Jason hurried from the room. Riki waited for a minute before joining him at the top of the stairs. She'd seen the tears in his eyes, and wanted to give him time to get a grip on his emotions. Her respect for him had just gone up another notch. She couldn't think what he must be going through, not even knowing he had a daughter until she was six. Then to throw all of Charlie's problems on top of that . . . She could only hope his shoulders could carry the weight.

"How about going to my study?" she asked. "I think we both can use a drink. Then we can talk."

Jason cleared his throat. "Lead the way. It sounds like a good idea to me."

Downstairs, Riki turned in the opposite direction from the kitchen. She slid open a pair of sliding doors made of oak and stained glass, revealing a magnificent room. Jason had never seen a room like it before. The cream-colored carpet had to be three inches thick. The walls were paneled in teak, and powder blue satin draperies were drawn across the windows. Logs lay in the marble fireplace, ready to be lit. In the center of the room was a huge antique desk with a leather swivel chair behind it.

Riki walked over to a wall that was almost completely covered by bookshelves. A cabinet stood in front of it. "What do you drink?"

"Do you have Scotch?"

"Yep. Ice?"

"No, thank you."

After fixing his drink and an apricot brandy for herself, she led the way over to the window that had two wing chairs and a table in front of it. She sat in one of the chairs and motioned for Jason to take the other. He sat down and stared at his drink. Riki decided not to bring up the subject of Charlie until he had relaxed somewhat.

"This is my sin room," she said.

"Your sin room?"

"Yes. This room is off limits to the kids. Isn't that awful that they aren't allowed in it?"

"Not really. This is exquisite. It must have cost you a fortune to do."

"It really only cost time, not money. When I bought the house, this room was just like this, except the paneling all had to be refinished. The fireplace needed some minor work, and I got a mason to do that. The desk and chair were in the attic. Can you believe that the former owners told me there was junk in the attic and I could throw out what I didn't want? When I think of the nights I spent on that desk . . ." She shook her head. "It's astonishing what some people think is junk."

"You refinished that desk?" Jason was truly amazed.

"I refinished just about everything in this house. It's my hobby. It keeps me from going nuts. A woman in town makes all my drapes, and she also upholsters most of the furniture for me. She's a widow and I tell myself she could use the extra money, but the real reason is I can't sew for a damn."

"Mrs. Perfect has a flaw?"

"Several."

"I must congratulate you. You really did an outstanding job on this desk. From the look of the rest of the house, you've done a bang-up job on all of it. But can I ask one question? Why didn't you do anything on the outside of the house?"

"I've been telling everyone that it's because of the weather, but now that it's spring that excuse won't hold. The real reason is my second flaw. I'm scared to death of heights."

"Considering this house is three stories high, you may have a problem." Jason was pretty sure Riki didn't tell everyone she was afraid of heights. He gave her credit for knowing her limits. Now he wondered how she was going to get around the difficulty.

"I sure do have a problem," she said. "The last time I was up on the third floor, I broke out in a cold sweat and had to stay in the basement for two hours." She shuddered, remembering the feeling.

"No offense intended, but I don't see how that helps."

"Are you scared of heights?"

"No."

"Then you wouldn't."

"Oh." Jason still didn't understand what the basement had to do with Riki being afraid of heights, but obviously she didn't want to discuss it anymore. He had no idea why they were discussing the house anyway. The only reason he was here was for Charlie. "Do you think Charlie will ever talk again?" It was the first question that came to his mind.

Riki looked at him as if trying to see into his soul. After apparently coming to a decision, she rose and crossed to the desk. She picked up a manila folder that was lying on top of it and handed it to him. "Here is the complete file on Charlie. It is as accurate and current as possible. Why don't you read it while I go make some coffee? I'll be back in a bit. Make yourself at home."

After Riki left the room, Jason sat there holding the file. His daughter's life was written on a few pages and stuffed into a folder. Not knowing what he was going to read made him nervous. Shaking his head as if to clear it, he opened the folder and started to read.

When Riki returned Jason was standing at the window. He held the drapes back with one hand. In the other hand was a fresh drink. From his rigid stance she could tell his thoughts were deep and troublesome. He hadn't even heard her enter. She carefully set the tray on the table and walked over to him. She wanted to cradle him in her arms and tell him everything would work out. But that was the million-dollar question. Would everything work out? From what she could make of the reports, something more than the death of her parents had traumatized Charlie. She was almost positive that whatever it was, it had happened before the tragic accident. Since Charlie wasn't talking, she had no way of finding out what it was.

Jason turned toward Riki, aware that all his doubt and confusion was reflected in his eyes. He felt so helpless. He was, he admitted, totally out of his depth. He knew nothing about children, especially ones with emotional problems. He had to leave everything in Riki's hands, or risk taking Charlie to another stranger for professional help. Of the two choices, he'd pick Riki. From what he had seen of Charlie, she seemed happy here. The reports he had just read indicated she was improving. She was accepting the social structure of the family. He couldn't remember the last time he hadn't been in control of a situation, and he didn't like the feeling at all. For Charlie's sake he would try to tolerate it.

He raised his glass and drained it in one swallow. "Okay, I read all the technical stuff. Now suppose you tell me in English what it all means."

Riki led the way back to the wing chairs and poured their coffee. After Jason had sat down and taken the cup, she cut to the heart of the matter. "The bottom line, as I see it, is Charlie is cutting herself off from everyone because, I believe, she feels guilty." At Jason's raised eyebrows, she clarified her statement. "I can't be one hundred percent sure, but I believe Charlie thinks she caused the accident that killed her mother and supposed father."

"How could she think that? She wasn't even there."

"You have to remember that you are dealing with a six-year-old child, not a rational adult. No one knows except Charlie what went on before the accident. From what I can gather, something did. I don't know what. Maybe her mother and father were fighting, and just maybe she was the cause of the argument. It is quite normal for parents to fight over a child. They could have been fighting in front of Charlie, or maybe she overheard them. Either way, the guilt was placed on her shoulders. The next thing she knew a social worker was telling her that her mother and father were dead. Hence, the total withdrawal. And who could blame her? From all the information we have, Charlie didn't know that Richard was not her father."

"So how do I tell her *I'm* her father, after six years? And how do we get her to talk?" He anxiously ran his hand through his hair.

"Time."

"How much?" He barked the question out of sheer frustration.

"As much as needed." Riki's voice lowered as her temper grew higher. "Need I remind you, Mr. Nesbit, that we are dealing with a very young child? Your child, to be more precise." She calmly placed her coffee cup on the tray, then gripped the arms of her chair. She was prepared to do battle, and she wasn't going to lose.

Jason took one look at her and grinned widely. He saw a flush start at her neck and creep up onto her face. Her eyes held more than a hint of anger. They were proclaiming death. He couldn't help himself any longer. He let out a roar of laughter that was so loud, he was surprised it didn't wake the kids.

"I'm sorry, Riki, but now I know why you have red in that gorgeous hair. You have the fastest temper I've ever seen. I'm not upset about how much time it will take Charlie to talk. I'm just very anxious for her, that's all. I know it's going to take time, and I have all the time in the world. So just simmer down and tell me what to do. I haven't the faintest idea where to begin."

Lord, she was beautiful when she was mad, he thought. Her eyes started to smolder and her face flushed. He wondered if she looked like that when she was making love. With that temper, there was passion there too. It would just take a certain man to bring it out—like himself.

"Thank you," she said.

"For what?"

"For saying my hair is gorgeous." Riki couldn't resist the impish smile she flashed at Jason. "Now to get back to the subject at hand, I don't think we should tell Charlie you're her father yet. I would like her to get to know you first, though that will be tricky. That means you will practically live here. You'll eat with us, drive her to school, maybe even help with homework, whatever it takes. I want Charlie to become used to you before we drop the bomb. The only problem is that you are going to have to put up with me and six other children."

"That will be no problem. I'll even volunteer to sleep here." Jason couldn't help that comment, it just popped out of his mouth.

Riki decided to ignore it. "I will feed you, do your laundry, and whatever else in the domestic department that is required. The only thing I ask is that you treat all seven children as equals. I know you would like to give special attention to Charlie, and you do have that right, but think how the other children would feel. They don't know that you are Charlie's dad, and they would be hurt if you played favorites. Jake and Pete don't need any upsets in their lives at this point. The adoptions will become final soon, but until then I'm sure there are doubts in their minds. You can spoil Charlie rotten as soon as she's in Texas."

"Okay, I can see your point. No favorites. Why do Pete and Jake have doubts? Don't they like it here?"

"I'm sure they love it here, but they don't understand why I would like to adopt them. Jake has been in more institutions and homes than I care to tell you. He was given up at birth and no one would adopt a blind child. All his life there was never anyone. I'm sure he is questioning why I would want a blind child.

"Pete started developing a hearing problem when he was two, but no one picked it up. He was already in a foster home at the time, and they didn't want a child who wouldn't listen. Neither did anyone else. Everyone thought he was either stupid or just plain bad. No one bothered to check out why he wasn't listening, until he came here. His last foster home was a real joke. I have already recommended that it be shut down. He had a mouth on him that could make a truck driver blush, and we had quite a few run-ins in the beginning. Neither one of the boys knew what love was. They were used to being last on the list."

"What about you? No doubts?"

"Plenty, like bringing the children into a family with no father. But I figure one parent is better than none."

"That's mighty unselfish of you."

"Unselfish? Nope. I always figured that the more love you give, the more you receive."

Riki noticed the strange way Jason was looking at her and decided to change the subject.

"Breakfast will be around eight in the morning, and you are invited to go to church with us." She stood and turned to pick up the tray, but Jason already had it. He followed her into the kitchen, where she rinsed out the cups. "Is there anything that you need or something that you couldn't find?" she asked as she led him out onto the back porch. She figured it was a lot safer to get Jason out of her house.

The night air was cool, and the only sound was the chirping of crickets. The porch was totally dark except where the light spilled from the windows of the house. Jason faced Riki. "There is one thing I need."

She turned from the view of the distant mountains right into Jason's arms. She had no time to do anything before his lips captured hers. Her hands came up to push him away, but never did. The kiss started out gentle and slow, but when Riki responded to his lips, Jason lost control, and fast.

He had only intended a friendly good-night kiss. He had been dying all day long to know the taste of her. Once he had her in his arms, though, all his good intentions flew out of his mind. His tongue slowly outlined her lower lip, asking entrance. He felt her arms raise from his chest to circle his neck. One hand was running through his hair, while the other was pulling him closer. He heard her make a soft purring sound, then she opened her mouth to him. As the kiss deepened, he pulled her closer. He could feel her nipples hardening through the layers of clothes that separated them. His hands slid down her back to firmly cup her buttocks and hold her against him.

Riki was left in no doubt as to Jason's response to the kiss. It was pressed against the front of her jeans. She tried to get closer and found it impossible.

Jason slowly came to his sense. This was Riki he was kissing, he reminded himself. This was the woman who was acting as Charlie's mother. He slowly loosened his hold and started to break the kiss. Placing a few good inches between them, he cleared his throat. "I think we may have a problem here."

Riki gazed up into his eyes and couldn't think of one problem. Jason noticed her glazed, bemused look. He kissed the tip of her nose and turned her toward the door. "I'll see you around eight for breakfast." His voice was still husky and his breathing was uneven.

The last Riki saw of Jason he was slowly disappearing into the night.

Riki overslept the next morning, which was understandable considering she hadn't gotten to sleep before dawn. The vision of herself in Jason's arms kept her awake a long time. After losing practically a whole night's sleep, she still couldn't figure out what had happened.

She wasn't some schoolgirl who couldn't see what was on a man's mind. Jason definitely had had that hungry look in his eyes a couple of times yesterday. She hadn't been surprised that he'd kissed her last night. She had been surprised, if not downright shocked, by her response. She was a thirty-year-old woman, she had been married for over five years, and she had never once responded that way to a kiss.

Marriage to Brad had been comfortable, like being married to your best friend. In reality, Brad *had* been her best friend. They had rarely argued. Whenever there was a difference of opinion, they sat down and discussed it. Someone always compromised. Riki compromised on where to live. She wanted a home in a small country town, but Brad wanted to live in Richmond. They lived in Richmond. Brad compromised on children. Riki wanted a large family; Brad was content after the twins were born. After Andrew was born, Brad said they should call it quits. Riki wanted to try at least once more for a girl. Brad was killed in a car accident before he even knew she was pregnant.

The physical side had been comfortable too. Neither had placed excessive demands on the other. They had both been content, even if Riki never climbed to the heights that romance novels told her she should. She read what other women felt and laughed. Imagination was great, in its proper place.

Now she wasn't so sure. Maybe her response to Jason was because she hadn't been kissed in a long time. Especially by someone who looked like Jason.

A half an hour before he was due at Riki's, Jason was up and dressed. He glanced out of the window and spotted Travis and Trevor already out back. Both boys were dressed for church and were feeding the chickens.

Deciding that Riki must be up and about, he walked next door. Travis and Trevor had just finished and met him on the back porch.

"Hi, boys. Is your mom up?"

"Yep, she's in the kitchen."

As the three made their way to the kitchen, Jason could smell coffee and bacon. He stopped and leaned against the doorjamb. He noticed Charlie sitting at the table with the ever-present Tiny curled up at her feet. He couldn't stop the grin that spread across his face.

There was Riki dressed in an old football jersey that came to midthigh. Her hair was still tangled from sleep, hanging halfway down her back. She was barefoot, and he saw her toenails were painted pink.

She was trying to balance two cartons of eggs and a pitcher of orange juice. He pushed away from the door to give her a hand.

Riki noticed the movement from the corner of her eye, and made the fatal mistake of looking. The pitcher started to sway and orange juice splashed all down the front of her. The cartons of eggs slid forward. If it hadn't been for Jason's quick action, there wouldn't have been any eggs for breakfast.

He placed the cartons on the counter and turned toward Riki. "Good morning, Riki." His voice was low and intimate.

"You're early." Riki still held the pitcher, scarcely aware that the juice had soaked the front of her jersey. She was too busy staring at Jason. Lord, she thought, he was even better looking in a suit than in jeans. Most men looked uncomfortable wearing a suit. Jason wore one like he was born in it. She noticed that hungry look in his eyes again. He wanted to kiss her.

She would have given five years of her life to be alone in the kitchen with him. She kept telling herself it was just to see if last night's kiss had been a fluke.

"Riki," he whispered.

"Mmm?"

"If you don't stop staring at me that way, I will throw you down on the kitchen floor and make love to you. Audience or not!" The hungry look was replaced by something far more primitive.

Riki's first thoughts were of female bliss. To have this man make love to her would be heaven. In the next breath, the actual meaning of his words hit her. Good lord, what was she thinking? She hadn't even known this man for twenty-four hours and she was fantasizing making love with him on the kitchen floor.

She glanced quickly around the room to make sure they hadn't been overheard. Hastily putting down the juice, she mumbled something about getting dressed. She dashed through the doorway before Jason could respond.

He rescued the bacon before it burned. Staring at the eggs sitting on the counter, he started to chuckle. It was definitely going to be an interesting stay, but then again, he'd known that yesterday.

Riki didn't reappear until breakfast was half over. Jason was quite proud of himself. He had never scrambled eggs for nine before.

She was dressed in a crispy yellow dress with a scoop neck and buttons all the way down the front. There was a matching yellow belt around her waist, and on her feet were yellow sandals.

She had brushed her hair and left it loose, and he could detect a hint of makeup. She looked cool and sophisticated. He preferred her in the old football jersey, when she was hot and frazzled and not quite in control.

"I left your plate in the microwave," he said, smiling warmly. "I didn't know how long you would be."

Riki groaned silently. It only took one smile from him to have all her defenses come tumbling down. The pep talk she had given herself didn't seem to be working. If she was feeling this aroused in just a day, what would she be like in a couple of weeks. She'd be the one dragging him down on the kitchen floor. That would raise a few eyebrows. *Get your mind out of the gutter, Riki old girl, and appear to be intelligent.*

"Thank you, Jason. You didn't have to cook breakfast."

"Yes, I did."

For the first time since entering the kitchen, she looked directly at him. "Oh?"

"I was hungry." The look in his silver eyes told her it wasn't breakfast he was hungry for.

She didn't reply as she walked over to the microwave to retrieve her plate.

After breakfast with seven children, church was very quiet and relaxing, with all the children attending Sunday school. Jason sat with Riki. He didn't hear one word of the sermon. His whole concentration was on the pulse in her throat. Every time he brushed his thigh against hers, the pulse would pick up. She wasn't as cool as she would like to appear.

For some reason this pleased Jason considerably. He kept picturing her in her old football jersey with that look in her eyes. He could smell the perfume she was wearing. He could detect the fragrance of jasmine, but it was mixed with something else. Ten minutes later he turned to Riki and whispered, "Summer rain."

She looked around the quiet chapel. No one else noticed any rain. "What?" she whispered back.

"Your perfume. Jasmine and summer rain."

Riki stared at him. He looked like a boy who had just won the science fair. Good lord, she thought. He'd been sitting there analyzing her perfume. She quickly turned toward the pulpit, trying desperately to stop the blush.

Jason noticed the blush, but more importantly he noticed that pulse.

Three

Riki was relieved when the service was over and she and Jason were standing in front of the church. All she wanted to do was grab the kids and go home. Especially with the town gossips closing in on her. How was she going to explain Jason's presence? She couldn't tell the truth. It would be all over town within an hour. The chances of Charlie's finding out were too great.

Seven children barreled out of the church, coming to a screeching halt in front of Riki and Jason. Mrs. Ballinsky, the center of the town's gossip, was two steps behind them. Her face was red and flushed and she was breathing heavily.

Riki had to hide a smile, thinking that one of these days Mrs. Ballinsky was going to have a stroke trying to get the latest gossip.

"Good morning, Erika, children." She gave the children a quick glance, then dismissed them as unimportant. "And whom do we have here? A beau?" She was staring at Jason as if he had to be crazy.

Riki was just about to say he was an insurance salesman, when Andrew spoke up. "That's Jason. He lives with us."

Jason started to chuckle and Riki could feel the heated blush. She was never going to live this down. Mrs. Ballinsky drew herself up to her full height of five feet and two inches and puffed out her chest. "Well, I never. Erika, what kind of example are you setting for these poor children?"

Jason jumped right in. No one was going to insult Riki. "Riki is setting a very good example for her children. For your information, I am staying next door to Riki's for the next couple of weeks. I am a friend of hers, and I don't like it when you jump to the wrong conclusion and insult her like that. If you want answers, just ask a question. I figured you had more sense than to take a four-year-old's statement at face value."

Riki couldn't have said a word if she had wanted to. This was going to be worse than she'd thought. The whole town would start talking about her and Jason. Could any of this gossip upset the adoption proceedings?

"I'm sorry, Mister . . . ?" Mrs. Ballinsky looked at Jason, waiting for a reply.

"Nesbit, Jason Nesbit." He'd seen Riki stiffen, and decided for her sake to be nice to this busybody.

"Mr. Nesbit, I didn't mean to insult Erika or you. It just came as a total shock when Andrew said that you were living there." Mrs. Ballinsky glanced at Riki to see if she had accepted the apology.

"That's quite okay, Mrs. Ballinsky. I'm sure it

was a shock." Riki gave what she hoped was a smile.

"Well, I really must be going. One question, Mr. Nesbit. Just what kind of friend are you?"

"Riki and I have been pen pals for two years." Jason smiled innocently. "I figured it was about time I met her in person, so I took time from work, and here I am."

Riki started to choke. Jason patted her on the back.

"Pen pals. Isn't that the most romantic thing I've ever heard?" Mrs. Ballinsky smiled at Jason. "I've got to run. See you around, Mr. Nesbit. You too, Erika." She turned to the first group of ladies that caught her eye and walked rapidly toward them.

Riki glared at Jason. Her eyes were all watery from the choking spell. "Pen pals?"

"It was the first thing I could think of." His voice took on the high nasal sound of Mrs. Ballinsky's. "Isn't it sooooo romantic?"

Riki's eyes turned murderous. "I'm going to kill you, Jason."

"Here? Right in front of the poor children, Mrs. Ballinsky, her friends, the reverend?"

She scowled, then turned and marched away. She was halfway to the van when she stopped suddenly. She threw back her head and started to laugh. The more she thought about it, the more she laughed.

Jason's arm slid around her and he drew her close. "Does this mean I'm forgiven?" he whispered in her ear.

"Of course. I've never had a pen pal before." She

slipped out of his hold and raced the kids to the van, screaming, "Last one in is a rotten egg."

After a very hectic lunch and a quick change of clothes, everyone piled back into the van to go to ball practice. Jason couldn't help chuckling at the picture they made. It was like car-pooling with midgets. He was still amazed at the cooperation the kids gave one another. They had the system down pat. Travis always helped Jake when he needed it. Everyone pitched in with Billy-Jo, even Charlie.

As they drove to the field, Jason kept smiling as he remembered Riki rushing down the stairs. She was wearing faded jeans, sneakers, and the team's blue T-shirt. It read 'Coach' across her chest. She had her hair pulled back in a ponytail that hung out of the back of her baseball cap.

His full attention was on the word 'Coach' as she bounced down the steps. When she stopped next to Jason, she knew perfectly well what he was staring at. She made a mental note never to run down the stairs again when Jason was around.

"Coach?" His voice was low and husky.

"Yep. Someone had to do it. All the dads seemed to have other things to do." She smiled and blew a gigantic pink bubble. It burst with a loud pop. She pulled it off her face and popped the gum back into her mouth. Grinning saucily, she said, "I can't stand chewing tobacco."

"Thank heaven for small favors." He was chuckling as he pulled a piece of gum off her nose. He held it up, wondering what to do with it.

Riki didn't know what possessed her at that moment. She reached up and sucked Jason's finger into her mouth, her teeth pulling at the gum.

With his finger still between her lips, she slowly lifted her gaze to his.

There was no mistaking the look in Jason's eyes. She was sure the same look was in her own. She had no idea how long they stood there staring at each other before she slowly released Jason's finger. She couldn't stop the small sigh that escaped from her lips.

His head started to descend and she knew he was going to kiss her. She made no move to prevent him. She wanted him to kiss her.

The slamming of the back door sounded like a shot. Jason jumped back, and Riki blinked.

Travis skidded into the hall. "Mom, are you ready yet?"

"Coming," She answered. Avoiding looking at Jason, she started for the back door.

She got two feet before the sound of Jason's laughter froze her in midstride. How dare that man laugh at her? She could feel the heat of humiliation on her cheeks as she slowly turned to face him.

Jason knew he had made a mistake the instant he saw the murderous gleam in her eyes. He also knew she had put the wrong meaning to his laugh. Good lord, was she crazy? he wondered. Why would he laugh at what had almost happened? He had never felt this instant attraction before. He had a gut feeling that neither had Riki.

He glanced around to make sure they were alone, then grabbed her by the shoulders and placed a hard swift kiss on her lips. She blinked in surprise. That wasn't the reaction she had expected.

"Before you fly off the handle, Riki, let me explain. I was laughing at the back of your shirt.

How did you get stuck with a team named 'Farley's Funeral Home'?"

She glanced over her shoulder as if trying to read the back of her shirt. "Oh!" She turned back toward Jason with a guilty look. "Just lucky I guess."

He opened his mouth to say something, but the slamming of the back screen door stopped him.

"Mom, are you coming?" Andrew asked, running down the hall at top speed. Jason made a wild grab for him as he sped by. Lifting Andrew straight into the air, he carefully sat him on his shoulder.

"Yes, your mother is coming, young man." As he ducked through the back door, Riki was sure he mumbled something to the effect of "I wouldn't miss this for the world."

She stuck out her tongue as the man and the small boy on his shoulders made their way to her van.

As Riki parked the van Jason glanced at the six kids tossing balls back and forth in the field. They were obviously on Riki's team. They all had 'Farley's Funeral Home' shirts. Jason wasn't an expert, but anyone could see they were having trouble catching the ball.

As the kids and Tiny unloaded from the van, Riki pulled open the rear doors. Jason came around the side of the van as she was struggling with a huge duffel bag. He moved her aside and lifted the bag.

She made a face at him. "Make yourself useful." She watched him carry the duffel bag toward the dugout. She couldn't help noticing how his muscles tensed to handle the weight of the bag. He tossed it to the ground as if it weighed next to nothing. Every time she carried it, she practically got a hernia.

She dumped the contents of the bag near the dugout. Four of the kids who had been playing catch grabbed the bases. They ran out onto the field and positioned them.

Riki clapped her hands to get everyone's attention. "Okay, team, I would like you to meet Jason Nesbit. He's a friend of the family. He has graciously consented to help coach you guys while he's in town."

The cheers were deafening. Jason glanced at Riki to see her reaction to the boys' obvious relief. She was smiling at them. "Yeah, I figured that would be welcome news." Laughing, she continued, "Now, Jason can't remember all your names today, so help him out. Okay?" The boys nodded. "All right. Get your gloves and take your positions. I'll hit you a few to warm up. This way Jason can see where you need improvement."

She picked up two balls and a bat and headed for home plate. "My glove is right there, Jason. You can borrow it." She tossed her head in the direction of an old glove.

Jason noticed that Charlie, Andrew, Jake, and Billy-Jo were seated in the dugout. Tiny's head was resting in Charlie's lap while she scratched behind his ears. Jason smiled and waved.

He was turning back to the field just as Riki threw a ball straight up and slammed it. The ball went deep into left field. Damn, could she hit! he thought. The boy playing left field fumbled it.

After she got the ball back, she clobbered it again, this time to right field. Once more, the outfielder dropped the ball.

She continued this pattern until every boy had had a chance. Jason noticed most of the boys bobbled the ball. He hoped their hitting was better than their catching.

He had a perfect view of Riki's sweet tush as she bent over to set up the practice tee. What he wouldn't give to be a pair of jeans at that moment. He mumbled a curse and shifted his position. Damn, he'd be teaching these boys more than baseball if he kept thinking that way.

By the time he had cleared his mind of ludicrous thoughts, Riki already had the boys starting their batting practice.

He noticed that no one really had any trouble batting. Only one little boy named Tommy seemed to have a problem running. Jason had noticed a slight limp while Tommy was playing third base.

It looked like catching was what they needed to concentrate on.

After everyone had gotten his chance to bat, Riki called them all in. They gathered around Jason with eager anticipation on their faces. He hoped they didn't expect miracles from him. He had never even seen a T-ball game, let alone coached one.

"Okay, guys, it looks to me as if you could do with some catching practice. Travis, please give your mom your glove and we'll show you how it's done."

"But, Jason," Travis sputtered. At Jason's raised eyebrow, Travis handed over his glove.

Riki handled the glove as if she expected it to

bite. "Jason, I think there's something I should tell you." Her voice was low and hesitant.

"Riki, if you want me to help coach, please stand on first base like a good girl."

There was an outbreak of chuckles and snickers from the boys. Jason pinned them with an icy glare. He shouldn't have talked to Riki that way, he thought, but she had asked for his help. He didn't notice Riki walking toward first base as if it were the guillotine.

"Now," he said to the boys, "I'm going to throw a high pop to Riki. Watch how she gets right under it. Always keep your eye on the ball."

He threw the ball, and Riki positioned herself right under it. The next instant he couldn't believe his eyes. As the ball started to descend, Riki closed her eyes. Both her arms shot up to cover her head. The glove still faced outwards, as if the ball were going to fall into it.

The ball dropped harmlessly in front of her. Riki slowly lowered her arms and glanced at Jason. To say he was dumbfounded would have been an understatement. His mouth was hanging open so far, she was sure his jaw was unhinged. She waited for the shouting to begin, but there was only stunned silence.

Then the boys started giggling and laughing. She was sure they were laughing at Jason's face, not at her catching. They all knew she was scared to death of the ball.

In the next instant it was Riki's turn to be stunned. Jason let out a roar of laughter and promptly plopped his butt in the dirt. He was laughing so hard, he was holding his sides. Tears were rolling down his cheeks. He wiped his eyes with the back of his hand, leaving behind a streak of dirt.

He looked again at Riki and let out another roar. He fell backward in the dirt, still laughing. Riki picked up the ball and marched toward him. The boys gathered around Jason as if to protect him.

She wanted to wrap her hands around Jason's throat for laughing. But then again she had to be nice to him so he could teach the boys how to catch.

Jason glanced up and saw a furious Riki standing over him. He tried to swallow back another laugh, but there was no way he could stop his shoulders from shaking.

Riki noticed he was trying to control his mirth, even if he was failing miserably. She reached out a hand to help him up. "Does this mean you're willing to help coach?"

He took the hand and slowly stood up. He didn't trust that innocent expression on her face.

"Sure, I'll help coach." He glanced at the boys, blessing them for their presence. He didn't want to find out what Riki would have done if they were not there.

"Good," Riki said. She leaned closer and whispered, "Don't look now, but your zipper is down."

His hand flew to the front of his jeans as his face turned a dull red. When he realized she wasn't telling the truth, she was already heading for the dugout with an impish smile plastered on her face.

He had to suppress the desire to take her in his arms and kiss her senseless. That would have wiped the smile from her face. He liked that she fought back. That was a sure sign of passion. He also knew exactly where he wanted that passion directed.

It felt good to prop her feet up after a hard day, Riki thought. A gentle sigh escaped her lips as contentment settled in her heart. How she loved to relax in her lounge chair with a cup of coffee after all the kids were in bed fast asleep. The night air was turning cool, but she was too lazy to go retrieve a sweater.

She studied Jason from under her lashes and wondered what he was thinking. Was he remembering last night's kiss on this porch, or the cookout this evening? She closed her eyes and a vivid picture of Jason cooking appeared in her mind. He was standing in front of the grill with his head bent toward Charlie, patiently explaining the merits of his secret chicken barbecue sauce. Riki had jumped at the chance of Jason's help with dinner. Barbecuing was not her forte. For the two years that she had lived here, the fire department had responded four times to her cookouts. The fire chief had personally bought her her own extinguisher, especially designed for barbecues.

To give Jason credit, he really did try to hold back his laughter when Travis brought out the extinguisher. But when Travis and Trevor started to relate past cookouts with all the zest and gore of war stories, his control broke. It wasn't her fault no one had ever explained to her how much lighter fluid to use. The flames weren't quite as high as Trevor indicated, though. By the look on

Jason's face, one would believe that 747's had to be detoured around the area while she cooked.

She felt it had been childish of Jason to remove her bodily from the backyard. To be relegated to the kitchen in charge of potato salad and iced tea had seriously injured her pride. Of course, sticking out her tongue and making rude noises at Jason's retreating body had boosted her pride back up.

She assigned Charlie to be the assistant chef in charge of barbecuing. Pure happiness shone in the girl's eyes. As Charlie and Tiny walked toward the backyard, Riki couldn't help grinning like an idiot.

If the amount of leftovers was a sign of how much everyone enjoyed themselves, the barbecue was a success. There weren't any. Riki had to admit that Jason's secret sauce was sensational. She'd also conceded he was the better chef, since no firemen showed up for the feast.

The only odd thing that happened was Charlie's behavior. She seemed delighted to help Jason cook the chicken. That in itself was a breakthrough. Charlie had never been delighted about anything until Jason showed up. What really raised Riki's eyebrows was that Charlie practically climbed on Jason's lap to eat her dinner.

Jason smiled at her and piled more potato salad on her plate. Riki realized he didn't understand the significance of Charlie's actions. For that matter, Riki herself was having a hard time trying to decipher them.

Thinking of Charlie and Jason, Riki decided she had better get her mind back to the present.

She still had to say good night to Jason without a recurrence of last night's kiss.

She opened her eyes. Jason was drinking his coffee and looking out at the peaceful night. She shifted her gaze to the mountains in the distance and thanked God for seeing her through another day. With seven kids, she figured it paid to keep in touch with the "higher" help.

Jason sipped his coffee while he studied the woman sitting quietly beside him. Riki. How could one woman be so complicated. She was a mother, a member of a church, an upstanding citizen, a coach. Now what kind of woman coached a boys' T-ball team, just because nobody else would, especially when she was terrified of the ball? She also did most of her own furniture refinishing, and had an outrageous sense of humor. Most importantly, she was a very passionate woman. The kiss from the night before was still fresh in his memory. Yes, sir, Riki was a very passionate woman.

He turned to her.

"So how did I do today?"

Riki was so startled, she almost spilled her coffee. The quiet night and cool air had helped her relax. She'd been nervous all day with Jason. After the way they had parted last night, she hadn't been quite sure how he would act. So far, he had been a perfect gentleman. After clearing her throat to remove the huskiness, she replied, "Fine."

"Just fine?"

At the hurt in his voice, she giggled. "No, Jason, you were wonderful. Thank you again for helping with the boys' T-ball practice. I can't tell you how much it means to them."

"My pleasure."

"You really shouldn't have bought everyone ice cream afterwards. I'm afraid they'll think they'll get it after every practice."

"I'll try to curb my generosity the next time."

"Jason, wipe the silly grin off your face."

"Yes, ma'am."

Suddenly her expression changed from the teasing smile to a doubtful frown. "Jason, something isn't right."

He straightened the chair he was leaning back on. His feet hit the wooden porch at the same time as the front two legs of the chair. "About what?"

"Charlie."

"What's wrong with her?"

Jason's voice was lower and harsher. His concern was evident, and so was the authority. This was the side of him she had only guessed at, but had known was there.

"Nothing's wrong with her. Don't worry. I didn't mean to upset you. It's just that Charlie is reacting differently than I figured."

"How?"

"I expected her to be shy, leery of you. You're a stranger to her. You show up on our doorstep one day, and the next she's accepted you as part of the family." Riki slowly shook her head.

"Well, I am her father."

"She doesn't know that. She thinks her father was killed in the car accident."

"Maybe she likes me?" There was a hopefulness in his voice that Riki couldn't miss.

"Oh, I know she likes you. I just can't figure out why." She knew she was baiting him. She just couldn't seem to help herself.

"Some women think I'm handsome." Now there was a definite growl to his voice.

"I'm sure some do, but don't you think Charlie is a little young yet to get her head turned by a pretty face?" Riki's voice was pure sugar.

"Some women like their men rich." The growling was louder.

"I guess buying the whole team ice cream can be counted as rich to some. You will have your work cut out for you, though, if Charlie learns that money isn't everything."

"Some women like their men experienced."

"In what?"

He slowly stood up and set his coffee cup on the porch railing. He turned to Riki and removed her cup from her hands.

Riki couldn't look away from him. How could so much soul-burning desire be contained in one pair of silver eyes? she wondered. "In knowing," he whispered, "how to make a woman's body come alive during lovemaking."

Her gaze lowered to Jason's mouth, and her mouth went dry. Her whole body was coming alive and he hadn't even touched her. She could feel her breasts swelling and her nipples hardening. There was a strange sensation in the pit of her stomach, not unlike the one she got from riding a roller coaster. The sensation was drifting lower as Jason was leaning closer. She knew she didn't want to get off this ride.

Her tongue darted out to moisten dry lips. "I think we got off the subject." It was a last-ditch effort to prevent the inevitable. Her voice was low and husky, and she couldn't stop staring at his lips.

"And what do you like in your men, Riki?"

She said the first thing that came into her mind. "Roller coaster rides."

She barely had enough time to draw a breath before Jason's lips covered hers. The kiss started out hungry, and his tongue plunged into her mouth. Her arms circled his neck, and she pulled herself deeper into the kiss. She wasn't sure who moaned. She thought it was Jason, but it could have been she. Last night's kiss was no fluke. Her reaction was the same—total surrender.

Jason's mouth left hers to blaze a trail down her throat. She arched her back to give him better access. He must have adjusted the arms on the recliner, because she found herself slowly sinking backward. His mouth made its way back up to her waiting lips, after a slight detour to a very sensitive spot behind her ear.

This time when their lips met there was tenderness and warmth. The passion and hunger were still there, just not as primitive. Riki found herself lying side by side with Jason on the lounge chair and couldn't figure out who was holding whom closer. Jason was placing kisses down her throat toward the V in her blouse. As he undid the first button, she couldn't prevent the small purr that escaped her lips.

As the second button came undone, she pulled his shirt from his jeans and caressed his bare back. She could feel warm skin and hard muscles as her hands slid upward toward his shoulders. His fingers were on the third button as his lips traced the lace of her bra. She instinctively arched her back, and he growled. The fourth and last buttons were undone with undue haste.

Jason raised his head to see how Riki was reacting. The look in her eyes set all his doubts to
rest. She saw his concern and smiled, her hand
moving from his back to his chest. She could feel
the rapid beating of his heart and the heat of his
body. She leaned over and kissed his neck. His
breathing became more labored and his hand trembled as he found the front clasp of her bra. The
bra came undone the exact instant their lips met.

The hunger was back in full force, with the
tenderness lying in the background. Their tongues
met and dueled. No one won, but no one lost.
Jason broke the kiss, sliding his mouth downward. The feel of Riki's unconfined breasts crushed
against his chest was more than he could stand.

He gently pushed the blouse and bra aside as
he gazed at her. The light from the kitchen window spilled in a soft glow onto the porch. His
breath caught in his throat at the sight of her
breasts. One word came to mind as he raised his
head to smile at her. "Perfect."

Riki barely heard the softly spoken word before
his mouth took her nipple. Her back arched, her
breath stopped, and the roller coaster whirled down
a hill. Jason's tongue circled the aroused nipple,
then he sucked gently. The force of the roller
coaster was making it hard to breathe. She pressed
closer to him as she tried to draw air into her
lungs. His mouth left the hardened nub, and he
trailed moist kisses down her body. Her hand
went to the back of his head to try to bring him
back. He obeyed, rubbing his cheek against her.
The slight abrasion of his beard heightened her
desire. As his mouth settled on her other nipple,

her hand left his head and slowly trailed down his side.

His sudden intake of breath proved he was just as aware of her hand stroking up and down his thigh as she was. His own hands were not idle. One was caressing her back as the other slid over her hips. His hand was moving in a sensual rhythm that matched the gentle sucking of her breast. The roller coaster hit another dip. He raised his head to look into her eyes, and the heat of his passion seemed to burn into her. "Riki?" he asked urgently.

She knew the question without being asked. She also knew the answer. She loved roller coaster rides, and she had never been on one like this before. "Please."

He growled low as his lips settled on hers. His hand moved to the apex of her thighs, and the roller coaster hit another dip.

"Mommy?"

The roller coaster slammed to a screeching stop. They both froze as the sound of Billy-Jo's voice penetrated the night.

Four

Riki had no idea how she managed to stand up, her legs were trembling so badly. She tried three times before she finally hooked the clasp on her bra, and with shaking hands managed to button her blouse. She had never felt so humiliated in all her life, necking on the back porch at her age. Who was she trying to kid? It was more than necking, a lot more. Damn, she had been about to let Jason Nesbit, a perfect stranger, make love to her on her porch.

Thank heavens Billy-Jo hadn't opened the door. How do you explain that one to a two-year-old? Hearing Billy-Jo call her name again prompted her to move. She couldn't look at Jason, even if her life depended on it. Staring at the screen door, she cleared her throat. "Good night, Jason. Breakfast is at seven-thirty tomorrow because the children have school." She hoped she sounded more in control than she felt. She opened the screen door and stepped inside. She thanked her lucky stars that

Jason was at least a gentleman. Not many men would allow a woman to leave without some type of comment.

Jason came out of his shock with a jolt. Riki had just wished him good night and slipped into the house. What in the hell had come over him? He had never acted like that with a woman. Not even when he was sixteen and had "Lusty Lois" in the backseat of his father's car. Taking a deep breath, he heaved himself into a sitting position and straightened his clothes. With elbows on his knees and his chin resting on his palms, he stared off toward the mountains.

What had gone wrong? he wondered. Everything had been fine. He had never had so much fun, or laughed so hard. He had been unsure around the kids in the beginning since he had only limited experience with children. His own nephews and niece had seemed to grow up overnight. He saw them occasionally for family dinners. His sister Stella was constantly on him about taking a vacation and slowing down. Maybe she was right. She was thrilled about Charleen and had wanted to fly up with him to collect her. He had explained about Charleen's not talking, and how Mrs. McCormick and the social worker from Texas had agreed it might be better if he became a friend first.

Riki, he thought. That's what had gone wrong. Nowhere in his mind had he ever considered what Mrs. McCormick was like, besides being capable of caring for his daughter. Charlie was his only reason for being here. Why couldn't he devote one hundred percent of his time to Charlie, instead of trying to get Riki into bed?

Good lord, that sounded cheap, both of himself and of Riki. He was a grown man who should be able to control his libido, not some lascivious teenager. And Riki was definitely not his type. She didn't play games. She wasn't part of the flash-and-dash group he was used to. The women he dated knew the score before the game was played. The only score Riki knew was in T-ball, for cripesake.

It wasn't that she was unsophisticated or a country bumpkin. She was down-to-earth, warm, and vividly alive. She not only met life head on, she actually went out looking for it. She was as foreign to him as toboggans are to Dallas. Maybe that was the attraction for him—to confront the unknown, to boldly go where no man had gone before. Riki was the last frontier. Now he was sounding like Captain Kirk.

Jason forced himself to consider his options. The first one was the safest. He could pretend the whole thing hadn't happened, avoid Riki like the plague, make friends with Charlie, and leave for Dallas as soon as possible.

The second option was an all-out hot-and-heavy affair. Grab the goods while the grabbing was good. Enjoy this extra benefit from the trip, and when Charlie had adjusted, take the first plane home. Only a couple of things stood in the way of that plan. The first was, he had never grabbed anyone's goods before. He believed in giving because it made the getting that much better. The second obstacle was going to be the temptation to slit his throat every morning for the rest of his life.

The third and final option was to calm down

and take this one day at a time. There was obviously something between Riki and him, an instant attraction, chemistry. Chemistry? Now that was a joke. It was more like spontaneous combustion. All they had to do was touch each other and the flames erupted.

There was no way he was going to walk away from her without exploring this phenomenon. First, he had to confront her and make her realize there was something between them. Second, he had to assure her he was not going to rush her. He'd let her set the pace. He only prayed that the pace she set would qualify for the Olympics.

When Riki came back downstairs, she was startled to find Jason leaning against the kitchen counter, drinking a cup of coffee. So much for being a gentleman, she thought. Obviously he was waiting for something. Well, he was going to have a long wait. After tucking Billy-Jo back into bed, she'd given herself a lecture on the subject of men. First and foremost, Jason was dangerous. She had never met a man who had such an overwhelming effect on her body and mind. He had only to touch her and all her defensive walls came crashing down. It had taken her over two years to build those walls and in a matter of seconds Jason could knock them down, clean to the foundation.

Riki never considered herself a promiscuous female, but since meeting Jason she was beginning to have her doubts. After Brad was killed, her main concern in life had been the children, especially the unborn child she was carrying. Moving to a small rural town had been her dream come true. She had been perfectly content to raise her four healthy children, and had been surprised by her reaction to Jake.

When an old college friend got in touch with her about possibly taking Jake as a foster child, she was intrigued. After meeting Jake, intrigue turned to enthusiasm, and she brought him home as soon as possible. He was just starting to interact with the other children when her friend called again and told her the heart-wrenching story of Pete. She took him in as well. While Jake was quiet and undemanding from fear of rejection, Pete was the opposite. He was loud and demanding, always trying to be the center of attention. If he wasn't in trouble, he felt no one cared.

In the middle of one of their confrontations, Riki noticed the hearing problem. After several visits to a specialist, Pete was diagnosed as having an eighty-percent hearing loss. An operation was out of the question, for fear it would cause permanent damage. The specialist was hopeful that with the current medical advancements, there would be a procedure in the near future that could restore part, if not all, of Pete's hearing. In the meanwhile, there was a hearing aid. With Pete's hearing restored to almost normal, his behavior improved dramatically. He started to interact with the other children, and seemed to favor Andrew.

Riki found that Jake and Pete filled a void within her she'd never known existed. Not only was she surviving in this crazy world, she was helping two less fortunate children survive also. One day she realized it wasn't enough for Jake and Pete just to survive. They had to belong. After a lot of soul-searching and many family discussions, she started the adoption procedures, and never looked back.

About six months ago the Child Welfare Department called about Charlie. They assured her it was temporary, only until they located her father. They feared that placing her in an institution would cause the small girl to retreat further. Riki had to agree. Since taking Charlie into her home would in no way jeopardize the application for adoption of Jake and Pete, she opened her arms to the forlorn little girl.

Tonight was the first time she ever regretted that decision. Charlie she could handle. It was the six-foot hunk with the hungry silver eyes that had her in a tizzy. How was she ever going to survive the next few weeks with Jason practically living in her house?

Standing in the doorway of her kitchen and gazing at that perfect male specimen, Riki felt the first flicker of fear. The fear was not of Jason, it was because of him. While she was tucking Billy-Jo in, she'd sensed another void. This one couldn't be filled with children or friends. Jason had opened this void, and only he could fill it.

Jason read the fear in Riki's eyes and muttered an obscenity under his breath. So much for the gold medal. He set his cup on the counter and picked up the other cup, holding it out to Riki.

At her raised eyebrows, he muttered, "It's a peace offering. I'm not going to jump your bones if you walk into the kitchen."

She entered the kitchen and accepted the cup, totally taken aback by this turn of events. She had expected to have to fight Jason off. She leaned against the counter, imitating his casual pose. Never having been in a situation like this before, she was totally out of her league. Her only hope was to follow his lead, and pray she didn't make a total fool of herself.

Her prayers were not answered as she choked on her first sip of coffee. It wasn't the coffee that made her throat close up, it was Jason's statement. "I really do want to make love to you."

She glared at him through tear-filled eyes, tears brought on by the choking and his pounding her between her shoulder blades. How could he be so gentle when kissing her and fifteen minutes later leave black-and-blue marks on her back? After blinking several times and getting her breathing under control, she finally realized Jason was asking if she was all right. Taking a step away from him, she managed a very hoarse "Fine."

He watched her take a tentative sip of coffee. When all of her parts seemed to be working, he decided to continue the conversation. "I just thought you ought to know."

Riki could feel the heat rise in her cheeks and silently cursed Jason for his ability to make her blush. "I wish you would stop talking like that," she mumbled to the floor. She couldn't bring herself to meet his eyes.

A gentle, callused hand firmly cupped her chin and forced her eyes to meet his. "I'm sorry, Riki, if my words embarrassed you, but you are going to have to face facts. The first one being that I want you more than any other woman I have ever known."

Jason knew that if someone were to tell Riki that her eyes reflected female pride just then, she would have hotly denied it till her death. A self-indulgent smile crossed his face. Nothing like showing the enemy your Achilles' heel, he thought.

"I wouldn't gloat too fast, darlin'. It's unbecoming, and I might let my basic male impulse take over."

"I have never gloated in my entire life."

"There's a first time for everything."

"Is there?"

"Yes." His thumb outlined her slightly swollen lips. At her indrawn breath, heat surged through his loins. Lord, how could one woman have so much power over his body?

Riki couldn't help staring at him. It was an experience to watch desire flare in those silver eyes. Could he really want her that much? No man had ever looked at her like that before, not even her husband. What would it feel like to be drawn into that desire? To feel Jason's hard body poised above hers, to feel Jason fill that void? Her eyes widened with the realization that she was having a sexual fantasy about the man in front of her.

And that man looked as if he were carved out of stone. He had squeezed his eyes shut, as though to block out some pain. One hand was still in midair, hovering above her mouth, while the other was gripping the counter top. She nearly reached out to him, but indecision and confusion held her back.

Jason was desperately trying to hang onto the bit of control he hadn't already lost. This wasn't what he'd had in mind when he'd waited for Riki to take care of Billy-Jo. He was going to give her the time he sensed she needed. But damn, she could at least help. She didn't have to look at him as if he held the secrets of the universe.

He opened his eyes slowly to stare into her very

confused green ones. The confusion answered quite a few questions. First, Riki did want him physically. Second, she wasn't sure what she should do about the attraction. Third, and most important, he was going to have to take a very cold shower tonight. The time wasn't right. Something down deep inside him, the very core of his being, was screaming at him not to push her.

"Darlin'," he said softly, "we will make love, make no mistake about that. The only question is when. That's going to be your decision. Of course, I plan on helping you reach that decision as soon as possible."

The tender smile on Jason's sensual lips made Riki totally indifferent to what he was saying. The words were registering in her brain, but it was the shape and movement of those lips that held her fascination.

Those lips could do for a woman what Rembrandt did for canvas. They could be as soft as a whisper or as ruthless as a storm, not asking for a response, but demanding it. Her tongue slipped out from between her teeth and slid across her bottom lip. Jason groaned and placed a few feet between them.

"Listen, darlin', I would love to do what your eyes are begging for tonight, but I think you need time to understand the ramifications. I don't want a one-night stand with you. I'm not sure exactly where we're headed. There's Charlie to consider, along with the other children."

When Riki didn't reply and only continued to stare dreamily at him, he muttered a very explicit curse under his breath.

"Oh, little darlin', you are making this extremely

difficult for me. I never had a woman go speech-less on me before. I think I'm flattered. But I have a feeling that as soon as your brain kicks in, I'm a dead man." He clasped her hand and walked her to the back door. "Now, darlin', I'm leaving, while I still have the ability to. I want you to think over everything I told you tonight. When you reach your decision I want you to tell me. No, I need you to tell me. You have to be as positive as I am, because there will be no turning back. Now, I want you to lock this door behind me, and go to bed and try to get some sleep. One of us should be rested in the morning and I know it won't be me."

He leaned down and placed a lingering kiss on her forehead. Then there was just empty space where he had been. Riki slowly closed and locked the door and leisurely made her way upstairs.

Her brain didn't kick in until she was in bed. "That no good arrogant son of a sea biscuit, he's a dead man!" She accompanied this statement with several blows to the innocent pillow next to her. How dare he insinuate that they would be making love as soon as she gave the word? What did he think he was, irresistible? Maybe he thought he was God's gift to women. He probably thought she was easy pickin' because she was a widow. Well, if he thought that, he had another think coming. She was.

Staring up at the ceiling, Riki wondered who she was trying to kid. She would have made love to Jason tonight. He was the one who called a halt. He sensed she wasn't completely sure and had put a hold on his desire. She had thought she had her hormones under control, and she had until he'd said that he still wanted to make love to her.

Talk about having your hormones kick into overdrive. They had accelerated at such a rate, they'd temporarily shut her mouth down. There she'd stood with her jaw hanging to her knees, listening to the most gorgeous man alive tell her he wanted her.

Riki buried her face in her pillow to suppress a groan. What must he think of her? Probably that she was a real country bumpkin. He hadn't seemed to be gloating when he left, though. He'd seemed to be suffering. She knew he could have made love to her tonight. She also knew he knew it.

Now what do you make of that? she mused. Wasn't that the sweetest thing? Maybe chivalry wasn't dead after all. Snuggling deeper under the quilt, Riki smiled as she drifted off to sleep.

The week that followed was the most bemused, confused week of her life. Jason pitched right in, as if he were a born parent. He chauffeured children to their bus stops. He helped coach T-ball after school. He even helped with homework. He never showed favoritism toward Charlie, though he was never far from her side. At times Riki caught him staring at Charlie as if he didn't believe she were real. She was confused by her own reactions to the emotions that crossed his face. She felt love, pride, pain, and anger.

She wanted to comfort the little girl whose tragic experience of losing her parents had made her so withdrawn, she refused to speak. And she wanted to wrap her arms around Jason and tell him everything would work out all right. Tell him that Charlie would come to love him as a father, and someday she would call him Dad.

She couldn't bring herself to interfere with his private thoughts, though. She couldn't offer the guarantee it would all work out. With her knowledge of psychology, she realized the human mind offered no guarantees. She could only hope that with time and understanding Charlie would respond to the love. Jason's presence did seem to have a positive influence on Charlie. The girl didn't actually dog his every step, but everywhere Jason went, Charlie was in the general vicinity. Once or twice Riki actually caught a smile flicker across the child's face.

On that first Monday after dropping the kids off at the bus stops, Jason helped Riki clean up the kitchen. When they were through, he looked around. He was a man born for action, and sitting around a house all day waiting for Charlie to get home from school went against the grain.

"So now what?" he asked.

"Now what?" she repeated.

"Now what do we do?" There was a slight drawl in his voice that could have put another meaning to the question.

Riki's cheeks pinkened as she thought of all they could possibly do. "About what?" she quietly asked.

"Ah, darlin', I know exactly what to do about that. All you have to do is ask. I told you I wouldn't pressure you into anything you couldn't handle."

She leaned her hip against the counter and dropped her gaze to his expensive sneakers. Then she allowed her gaze to travel up his worn blue jeans, pausing for a moment where muscular thighs stretched the fabric. She purposely locked her eyes right below his belt. The obvious bulge of his masculinity had worn the blue denim almost white. Her glance took in the trim waist and rock-hard stomach, his khaki shirt that fit like second skin. It stretched across his powerful chest and barely contained his thick biceps.

It took every ounce of willpower to keep her face expressionless, not to let Jason see what looking at his body could do to her. Her eyes finally lifted to his face, and the first thing she noticed was the dull shade of red that had spread over his cheeks.

Her first impulse was to rape and pillage. She wondered if she had any ancestors who had been pirates. The second impulse was a purely feminine desire to see how far she could push him. She tried to look cool and sophisticated, which was a neat trick since she was wearing faded blue jeans and an old T-shirt. The bare feet, the pony-tail, and the absence of makeup really added an elegant touch, she decided. She purposely dropped her gaze to his belt buckle again, then back up to his silver eyes.

The little imp inside her had her speaking before she knew she had opened her mouth. "What makes you think I can't handle it?"

At his sudden intake of breath, she realized the challenge she just issued. Her eyes locked with his, and they were both aware of the sexual tension that crackled between them. From the back of Riki's mind came the prayer that Kermit the Frog and Cookie Monster could hold the attention of Andrew and Billy-Jo.

The only thing that stopped Jason from taking Riki up on her offer was the small flicker of doubt in her emerald eyes. When they made love he didn't want her to regret one minute of it. "Beware, darlin'," he said, his voice low and husky as he struggled to calm his rapidly beating heart. "I'm only a man, and you are playing with fire."

Riki should have been relieved by Jason's integrity, but she couldn't help feeling disappointed that he didn't act the rogue and seduce her right there. Wasn't it every mother's fantasy to make love on the kitchen floor while her two toddlers watched *Sesame Street* in the next room?

In a matter of three days her fantasies had changed from wanting quiet children and a clean house to vivid sexual encounters with Jason. She had had fantasies about Brad, but they had consisted of quiet walks through the woods holding hands, horseback riding, drinking wine in front of the fireplace with all the kids asleep. Soft, peaceful fantasies.

Never had she had such explicit daydreams, all concerning Charlie's father, no less. She had only to close her eyes and a recurring vision appeared. She and Jason were in her brass bed, the pale satin sheets shimmering in the firelight that illuminated the room. Jason's back glistened with perspiration as he rose above her, ready to join their bodies. She always came to her senses just when her legs started to circle his hips.

The first time she awoke from a sound sleep with that vision planted in her mind, she cursed her cotton sheets, the fireplace that didn't work, and Jason. She spent the rest of the night tossing and turning, remembering the taste of Jason's lips on hers. The feel of his hands on her breast, the sound of his deep groan when she trailed her hand on his thigh.

Now when Jason brought up playing with fire, the image burst into her mind. She cursed the telling blush that flared in her cheeks while frantically trying to remember what she should be doing on Monday. Changing sheets and doing the laundry was the best she could come up with on the spur of the moment.

Five

It took Jason a couple of minutes to convince Riki he really wanted to help her strip the beds. The winning argument was that after being a bachelor, he had to become more domesticated if he were to make a proper home for Charlie.

Assigning Jason the job of stripping the boys' beds, Riki went into the girl's room. Billy-Jo and Andrew called her away to settle a squabble before she could start in her room. She returned upstairs to find Jason standing at the foot of her bed.

After piling all the boys' sheets and pillowcases in a heap in the hall, Jason had decided to check out Riki's sheets. With a little boy's smile and a big boy's curiosity, he'd walked into her room. His glance quickly took in hardwood floors, a huge oak dresser, oak tables, and a wing chair done in a fabric of variegated purple. The wallpaper boasted miniature violets while all the wood trim was stark white. White lace curtains fluttered in the morning breeze, which carried the scent of the lilacs that bloomed in the side yard. A brass screen stood in front of the fireplace, and a silk flower arrangement done in purples was on the mantle.

Within a few seconds he'd taken in the room and decided it was Riki. The object that caught and held his attention was the queen-size brass bed. The bed itself was worth a second look—it must have cost a fortune—but that was not what interested him. As he slowly walked toward the bed, he gazed at the pale lavender sheets, bed ruffle, and pillow shams. A patchwork quilt had apparently been kicked to the bottom of the bed while the sheets were twisted every which way. Obviously someone had had a difficult time sleeping last night.

The thought of Riki lying beneath that old-fashioned quilt with her hair spread out on the pillow had a definite effect on his body. He grasped the cool brass of the foot board as heat ran through his veins. His gaze was fixed on the unmade bed, but he was seeing Riki lying there in naked glory, her arms reaching for him. He had never wanted a woman as badly as he now wanted her. Here he was aroused just because he had seen the big brass bed she slept in. He closed his eyes as a groan escaped his throat and a shaft of heat crossed his loins.

Riki heard the groan and crossed the room to stand beside Jason. Seeing the grip he had on the footboard and his closed eyes, she became concerned. Tentatively touching his arm, she softly whispered his name. His eyes flew open.

It took Jason a moment to realize that the hand resting on his arm belonged to the real Riki, not just some fantasy. The anxiety that shone in her eyes brought him back to earth with a thud. He reached out a trembling hand to caress her cheek. "What's the matter?"

Her eyebrows rose in question. "You tell me."

Disgruntled at being caught staring at tangled sheets, he smiled sheepishly and muttered, "Nothing a cold shower couldn't cure."

Now what did a lady say to a comment like that? Riki wondered. She knew what she wanted to say, but she didn't think offering to scrub his back would win her any brownie points at this time. "I'll handle the sheets in here," she said. "You go hang up the load of wash that's in the washer."

She had the bed stripped and was on the way down the stairs when it occurred to her what she had just told Jason to put on the line—all of her "unmentionables."

As she entered the kitchen she glanced into the laundry area. The washer lid was up, the washer obviously empty. With a groan of dismay she turned to the window that overlooked the backyard. There was Jason in all his masculinity pinning her silk undies to the line. She could tell he was enjoying himself immensely. All her bras were in a neat line, followed by a half slip and a peach camisole. He was currently shaking out each pair of very brief panties in assorted pastels and pinning them to the line. He seemed to be studying each pair, comparing them with each other. His glance lingered the longest on the French-cut pink pair.

Her breath caught in her throat when he reached into the basket and pulled out the last item.

As Jason held up the last garment, he thought

of how much fun doing laundry could be. Riki's appearance was one of earthiness on the outside. She almost always wore jeans and T-shirts, pulled her hair back in a pony tail, and seldom wore makeup. The only time he had seen her in a dress was for church on Sunday. Who would have guessed at the very feminine attire beneath her casual clothes. Pink silk panties and T-ball practice just didn't seem to go together.

As he pinned a creamy yellow teddy to the line, the desire to see Riki in this teddy flashed through him. She must have worn it under her yellow dress on Sunday. He had sat next to Riki in that church and smelled jasmine and summer rain and she had been wearing "this" beneath her dress. He was thankful he hadn't known she'd worn "this," because he had a feeling he would have embarrassed himself along with her in that pew.

How could a man on the down side of thirty become aroused hanging laundry? All this domesticating was hell on the libido. He didn't see how housewives stood it. He'd better leave all this to Riki and concentrate on something physical, something to use up all his excess energy.

Riki wanted to paint the house, but was afraid of heights. If she would hang her own undies from now on, he'd paint the house. Carrying the empty basket back inside, he stomped into the kitchen to find Riki going through the freezer. A muffled, "What do you want for dinner?" reached his ears from inside the freezer.

"Whatever you have. I'm not a fussy eater." With a frown marring his face, he asked, "What color do you want the house?"

Riki, who had been hiding in the freezer because she didn't have the guts to face a man who had hung her intimate apparel, turned around and faced Jason. "Why?" What did the color of the house have to with anything?

"Because I'm not cut out to become domesticated."

"Why?"

"Because it's hell on a man's nerves," he roared.

For the first time she noticed how upset Jason was. His brow was drawn into a fierce scowl, a flush stained his cheeks, a nerve in his jaw was twitching. He seemed to have been enjoying hanging the laundry, she thought. What could have possibly gone wrong? Had she done anything to upset him? Totally at a loss as to how to answer that statement, she decided to go back to the original question. "Light blue."

"You want the house light blue?" She nodded. "What color trim?"

"Colonial blue and white. Why?"

"Because I need to do something. Since you are feeding me and my daughter, I will paint your house."

She couldn't argue with that, but she did have some say-so about the details. Besides, she was totally thankful she had someone to volunteer to go up a ladder. She wasn't one to look a gift horse in the mouth. "Okay, but I pay for the paint, and I help."

The stubborn tilt of her chin was almost Jason's undoing. A chuckle threatened to escape at the thought of Riki painting this monstrous house by herself. Seeing the chin thrust out, he decided it was a smart move to suppress that chuckle and to appear to take her seriously.

"I thought you didn't like ladders or heights."

He saw a flash of fear in her eyes before she averted her glance. "Okay, you go up there and bring me down the shutters. I'll sand and paint them. I can also do the porches." A pleased expression crossed her face at the thought of actually getting the house painted. Maybe having Jason around wouldn't be that bad after all, if she could just learn to keep her hands off him.

"If you aren't going to let me pay for the paint," he said, "the least I can do is help with the food bill. I tend to eat quite a lot when I do physical work."

She knew exactly what kind of physical work she would like him to do. Come to think of it, she mused, her appetite had increased since Jason showed up, and not for food. She gave him a considering look. "I don't know," she said. "I think you'll be getting the short end of the stick. If you do all the work on the outside of the house, I think I should do all the domestic end and foot the bill."

"No, I'll help out with the food bill. You handle the everyday things, and if you promise not to starch my shorts I'll even repair the broken windows on the third floor." He leaned against the counter, crossing his arms over his chest. A smile tugged at his mouth as he came to the conclusion that bickering with Riki was quite enlightening. He noticed that when she was in deep thought she chewed on her lower lip. When she felt threatened her chin went up a notch and her hands automatically went to her hips. He could definitely make a career of studying Riki.

She smiled impishly. "If I promise not to turn your T-shirt pink, will you hang new rain gutters?"

"I kind of like pink underwear," he murmured, thinking of the pair he had just hung on the line. "The rain gutters are negotiable. Do I hear a bid?"

"You can wipe that leer off your face, Nesbit. I am a lady. I wouldn't dream of doing 'that' for gutters. Now fixing chimneys is a different story."

Jason was still chuckling when Andrew and Billy-Jo came into the kitchen wanting something to eat. He excused himself so he could go outside and see what kind of tools she had in the garage.

He'd been there for over a week and the house was still not painted. Shutters and old rain gutters had been taken down, and window panes had been replaced. All the old paint had been stripped and a primer sealer had been applied.

Jason was concerned for the elderly homeowners in the neighborhood after Riki explained that there wasn't a reasonably priced contractor. McElroy's Construction was the only contractor in town, and McElroy was of the opinion that if you can retire, you can afford his price. Most of the elderly were on pensions and social security, which didn't leave a whole lot for luxuries such as housepainting, window replacement, and all the other jobs they were getting too old to handle by themselves.

Jason spent one afternoon fixing Mrs. Wilson's porch steps. She in turn baked his favorite dessert, chocolate chip cookies. The more time Riki spent with Jason, the more she admired and respected him. He was courteous, kind and patient with everyone he met, and especially with the children. He had a chest that could stop traffic.

The first time she saw him working outside without a shirt, she practically went into cardiac arrest. Bronze skin shone with perspiration in the morning sunlight. Faded jeans clung tightly to muscular thighs and buttocks. A few dark hairs dusted an irresistible chest that cried out for a woman's touch.

He never made mention of that night on the porch, always acting the gentleman. On several occasions, though, she caught the hungry look of desire in his eyes. If she had had a mirror, she would have seen the same look in her own.

By Sunday night Jason had resigned himself to the idea of a long wait both for Charlie and for Riki. His arms ached to hold Charlie, to somehow make up for the lost six years. His body ached to feel Riki, to hold onto the warmth and passion that flowed through her.

Every night they followed the same ritual. She and he tucked the boys in and wished them good night. Then they tucked Billy-Jo in with tickles and kisses. She was such a loveable scamp, Jason never felt awkward hugging her and noisily kissing her.

Riki always backed up after kissing Charlie, to leave Jason some privacy. For eight nights he gently brushed her hair back and kissed her freshly scrubbed cheek. This was perhaps the hardest moment of the day for him. The need to hold her was so intense, his knuckles would turn white from the fist he made.

On the ninth night, something happened that neither Jason nor Riki could explain. After Jason's good-night kiss, Charlie reached up and placed a small kiss on Jason's cheek. It was such a spontaneous action, Jason acted instinctively and wrapped her in a hug. Riki couldn't say who was more surprised, herself or Jason, when Charlie cuddled into the embrace. Jason's arms contracted around the slight figure as he silently gave thanks.

Riki leaned against the door jamb with tears in her eyes. She didn't know who she was happier for—Charlie for finally reaching out to another human being, or Jason for finally getting to hold his daughter. She had no idea what had prompted Charlie's sudden behavior, but she knew it was the first step in the long road ahead.

Minutes later Jason released Charlie and carefully lowered her back onto her pillow. After tucking the blankets under her chin, he gently traced her cheek and whispered, "Good night, sweetheart." And Charlie smiled. Not the ghost of a smile, but a full-blown grin.

Riki waited for Jason in the kitchen, giving him time to control his emotions and giving herself time to control hers. With her back toward the door, she was measuring out coffee. Suddenly she was grabbed from behind and swung up into the air. Coffee grounds went flying in 360 different directions. Her protest died on her lips when she saw Jason's face. Pleasure radiated in the flush on his cheeks, and his little-boy grin was firmly in place. But his eyes told the story. Happiness shone in their depths, not just an outward happiness but an inner joy that could not be suppressed.

She was on her second spin in the air when it hit her. *I love him. I love Jason. I love a Texan.* What in the world was she going to do? But was it really love, or was it lust? True, Jason hadn't kissed her or touched her since that night on the porch, but she couldn't forget the delectable sight of him without his shirt on.

Being spun around in circles was making her dizzy and even more confused. Jason gently lowered her to the floor, a look of tenderness in his eyes. She knew he was waiting for her to make the next move, and for the life of her she couldn't decide what to do. The woman in her wanted to make love to Jason, while the mother in her was screaming to be cautious. Could she possibly become lovers with Jason without it affecting the children? What if they became too attached to him? Would having a lover jeopardize adopting Jake and Pete? Would it have a negative effect on how Charlie viewed Jason as her father? There were just too many unanswered questions. She would simply have to play Scarlett O'Hara and think about it tomorrow.

Jason could read the torment in Riki's eyes and knew tonight wasn't going to be the night. Even if she asked, he'd have to say no, as long as he sensed a second's doubt or hesitation. Over the past week he had read numerous emotions in her eyes—amusement, laughter, sadness, intelligence, and love. The last emotion was always directed toward the children . . . until tonight. If he wasn't mistaken, Riki was finally realizing what he figured out a few days ago. They were falling in love.

He wanted forever. He wanted Riki for his wife. He wanted seven children, and possibly another one of their own. He wanted the mountains of Virginia and he wanted this enormous house.

Caution seemed to be Riki's middle name, however. He had been on his best behavior so as not to scare her into thinking he was only after a quick roll on her brass bed. Endless nights of cold showers weren't helping his disposition, but what was one more night?

The need to put some distance between himself and Riki tonight was the major consideration now. The thrill and heartfelt relief he'd experienced when Charlie reached out to him would have to be celebrated in solitude. Having his emotions in such a turmoil was a new and frightening sensation, and he couldn't trust himself to call an end to anything physical tonight if Riki indicated she wanted more than friendship.

Two Scotches and a cold shower later Jason cursed himself for being so self-righteous. Staring at the ceiling while lying in a lonely bed was a terrible way to end an evening.

A few hundred yards away that very same thought was filtering through Riki's mind. Why did Jason have to be such a gentleman? Why didn't he make that first move? She wouldn't have resisted. For that matter, she would have welcomed him with open arms. He'd given his word, though, that she had to make the first move. Well, how in the hell did a woman go about seducing a gentleman? Say "please"? Did she say, "Come here, big boy. I want to feel your chest. How about after the kids are in bed and the coffee is perking, I slip into something more comfortable, like that creamy yellow teddy?" How was that for obvious?

Riki closed her eyes and told herself to relax. As she snuggled deeper under the quilt, she took a closer look at the situation. She was in love with Jason. He was only here for a short time, then he'd go back to Texas with his daughter. Nothing permanent could ever come from their love. He lived and worked in Texas while she raised her family in Virginia. If she was smart she'd send Jason and Charlie packing in the morning.

If Riki believed one thing in life, it was to live with no regrets. She couldn't picture herself at eighty rocking on a front porch and wishing her life had been different. A person should go out and do what she wanted to and live with the results.

Given the choice of either loving Jason and never knowing the ecstasy of his physical love, or sharing the greatest union a man and woman could know, she'd pick the greatest union, as long as it didn't affect Charlie, the adoptions, or her own natural children.

Two hours and a multitude of mumbling later, she decided that tomorrow, come hell or high water, she was going to seduce Jason. She was going to be the most seductive, captivating female he had ever laid eyes on. Now that would be some trick with seven children around. A satisfied smile lingered on her lips as she drifted off to sleep dreaming of ways to seduce Jason.

Jason had a difficult time breathing the next morning. Every morning, except the first one when he'd caught her in the old football jersey, Riki had been dressed by the time he arrived for breakfast. This time when he walked in the back door and spotted her cooking, he went into respiratory distress. She was wearing a mint green satin robe that barely reached midthigh. Her feet were bare and her hair was slightly mussed, as if she had just gotten out of bed. She glanced up from the frying pan and flashed a warm smile at him, and he felt his stomach nose dive down to somewhere around his left ankle. He'd always thought women were supposed to look their worst in the morning. If this was her worst, he was a dead man. How could she possibly look so kissable while making breakfast for him and seven children?

He looked around the kitchen. Travis and Trevor were arguing about whose shirt was whose. Andrew and Peter were fighting about whose turn it was to get the toy in the bottom of the cereal box. Jake was feeling the cereal boxes as if he could tell what kind was in which box, while Billy-Jo was sticking Fruit Loops in her hair. He noticed Charlie's hand disappear under the table for the third time and concluded that Tiny liked Cheerios.

How could all this be going on while he wanted to make love to their mother was beyond him. After seeing Riki in that robe, he was incapable of a coherent thought. He fixed himself a cup of coffee and carefully walked over to the table.

Riki placed a plate filled with pancakes in front of him. "Sleep well?" she asked huskily.

As she sat directly across from him, he couldn't help but notice the gaping lapels at her throat. Good lord, he thought. Did she have anything on under that? If she did, it surely wasn't much.

He managed a choked lie. "Like a baby."

Riki couldn't help but be a trifle disappointed by his answer, even if his voice did sound funny. "That's good," she said. "All I did was toss and turn." She admitted that stretched the truth a mite. After she had made up her mind to seduce Jason, she'd slept—like a baby.

She forgave herself the truth-stretching, though, when she saw Jason's reaction. He was staring at her, his fork midway to his mouth, desire flaring in his eyes. Her spirit lightened with the knowledge he wasn't as unaffected as he was trying to pretend.

With the five older children running around the kitchen trying to jam their books and lunch pails into their book bags, Riki made one last move. She leaned across the table to hand Jason a pottery pitcher and purred, "Maple syrup?"

The mouthful of pancake Jason had just eaten lodged in his throat and he started to choke. Taking a mouthful of coffee to wash it down, he wondered how those two words could sound so provocative. Images of Riki purring into his ear raced through his poor demented mind. He had to get out of there, immediately, before he made mad passionate love to her. All because she offered him maple syrup.

He abruptly stood up and summoned the kids. "Let's go, guys. We're going to be late."

Amidst all the confusion of kids racing for the door and Andrew and Billy-Jo begging to come along, Riki sat there calmly drinking her second cup of coffee. Jason ran his hand through his hair while hustling all seven kids and Tiny out the door.

A smile curved Riki's mouth. She had him on the run. Now for phase two. Tonight after dinner she was going to pull out the main artillery. After all, all was fair in love and war. As she climbed the stairs trying to decide which pair of shorts showed off her legs the best, she began singing Patsy Cline's "Sweet Dreams."

Jason knew it was safer to put some distance between him and Riki, and he decided to start painting the peak of the house that morning. It proved to be an almost fatal mistake. He nearly lost his footing on the ladder when he caught sight of her bending over the laundry basket. She had on a pair of dark blue shorts that left little to his imagination. As she straightened up, she turned toward him and waved. The motion drew his eyes to her breasts, clearly outlined in a white T-shirt that proclaimed Virginia is for lovers. Clamping his jaw shut, he waved the brush in response and turned back to the painting.

He angrily swiped the brush across the clapboard siding, splashing more paint on himself than on the house. For cripesake, he thought, he was only human. How much more was he supposed to take. If she was trying to give him a message, it was coming in loud and clear. Maybe all of this was innocent. After all, she'd only asked how he slept and offered him maple syrup. How could that be conceived as a come-on? For that matter, Riki didn't seem to know how to make a come-on. Maybe that was the problem. Maybe, just maybe, she wanted to take the relationship another step and didn't know how. He had told her the next move was hers. What if she was too shy to make it?

Taking another look down, he watched Riki finish hanging the laundry. It wasn't her fault the line was filled with pastel panties, bras, and two teddies—one in mint green that matched the robe she wore this morning and one in ice blue. How could a woman who wore those tiny scraps of lace be shy?

He had practically finished painting the side of the house before Riki called him for lunch. She, Billy-Jo, and Andrew were sitting at the picnic table on the back porch, and he joined them after he managed to clean most of the paint from his body. He nearly choked on his ham and cheese sandwich when Riki passed him the potato chips and batted her eyelashes. An idea was beginning to form when he felt her bare foot brush across his ankle. He glanced up in time to catch her whisper, "Excuse me."

Riki wasn't sure who was more surprised, she or the kids, when Jason threw back his head and roared with laughter. A flush started to creep up her cheeks at the thought that Jason felt her attempts at flirting were so funny.

Jason noticed the embarrassment she was suffering and winked. Her smile lit up her whole face. He couldn't tell what relieved him more—that Riki had decided to take the relationship further, or that his hormones weren't going crazy after all. They were just responding to her flirting. What endearing flirting it was too. He'd never had a woman actually flutter her eyelashes at him before. Her lack of experience was showing, but that only made her more enchanting, more desirable. If she wanted to try her wiles on him, he'd more than gladly sacrifice himself. And he knew that when the sun went down and the children all fell asleep, he had a few wiles he would like to try out on her.

Six

By dinnertime Jason had barely finished the side
of the house. Every few minutes he felt Riki's gaze
on him and he always returned the fascinated
looks. She had the most provocative eyes he had
ever seen. They seemed to bewitch and entice
him. They promised paradise. He came to the
conclusion that Eve must have had emerald eyes
and that they had held that look when she offered
Adam the forbidden fruit.

Riki couldn't remember what she cooked for
dinner, but since no one complained she guessed
it was all right. She did remember looking into
silver eyes and seeing a hunger that matched her
own. Everything was going to be fine, she thought.
Jason had understood her message. He'd showed
up for dinner freshly showered and shaved. She
couldn't decide if she preferred him shaved or
with a five o'clock shadow. He was dressed casually in jeans and a striped polo shirt that clung to
his chest. He seemed to push around the food on

his plate as much as she did. Did that mean he was nervous too?

Before dinner Riki had showered and washed her hair. After applying just a trace of makeup, she'd brushed her hair until it shone. She'd pulled on her sexiest pair of panties and tight-fitting jeans, and was relieved to see she didn't look bad for a mother of four. She slipped on an emerald green silk blouse that matched her eyes, sprayed on her favorite perfume, then took a last glance in the mirror and undid another button. What the heck? This was war. She was no Dallas beauty. She had to fight fire with fire.

All Jason could think about as he pushed his peas from north to south on his plate was, *My lord, she doesn't have a bra on.* Every time he looked up he couldn't fail to read the message in her eyes. Tonight was the night. All her uncertainty was gone. She was a woman who knew what she wanted and she was out to get it. He was all for that, except there were seven children in the room with them. Why didn't kids go to bed at a decent time?

When Charlie hugged him good night again, it almost snapped his control. Everything was finally coming together, he thought. His daughter was starting to trust him, the woman he was falling in love with was willing to reach for him as a man. How lucky could one guy get? Patience was the key to both women in his life. Just a little while longer and everything he wanted in life could be his. *Slow and easy, Jason, slow and easy.*

When he had finished tucking Charlie in, he met Riki in the hall. With a look of affection and something else that was hard to define, she whispered, "Why don't you go down to the study and fix us both a drink? I'll be right there."

He watched her hips sway as she walked into her bedroom. Knowing that he couldn't follow her into that room didn't help matters. A drink was in order, especially when he thought of the big brass bed in Riki's room.

He was on his second drink when Riki entered the study. He wasn't sure what to expect when she came down. He wouldn't have been surprised if she had slipped into something more comfortable. Her attempts at seducing him were only endearing her to him more. When she returned with no visible change, he decided that wasn't the reason.

He would have changed his mind if he had seen Riki staring at the mint-colored teddy. Should she or shouldn't she? she'd wondered. She was supposed to be a mature adult. This would be the first time she would make love to a man who was not her husband. Yet what if she had been reading Jason wrong? What if he had changed his mind and did not want her anymore? Wouldn't she look like a fool standing there in a teddy? Did men really like teddies? He seemed to find them fascinating on the clothesline. She hoped they looked better on her. Oh, the hell with it all, she decided. He would get her as she was. If he wanted her out of these clothes, he could just take her out of them.

When she entered the room, Jason handed her an apricot brandy, then calmly sat down in one of the wing chairs. Taking her cue, she sat in the other chair and sipped her drink. *Okay, Riki, old gal*, she told herself, *this is it, the big time. Do something.* The only thing she could come up with was to stare at Jason.

Jason glanced at Riki and could barely drag his eyes away. The hunger was there along with the need. She was his. All she had to do was say something to release him from his promise.

The tension in the room was electrifying. The hair on the back of Jason's neck was standing on end. This was the night. He could tell by looking into Riki's eyes. She wasn't going to say no, and she wasn't going to regret it in the morning.

If she didn't stop staring at him he'd go out of his mind. Her eyes were begging him to do something, but he couldn't. He'd promised her he wouldn't kiss or touch her unless she asked. He might be a perverted, deprived sexual maniac who couldn't control his primitive urges, but above all he was a gentleman. And gentlemen do not break their promises.

He finished his Scotch in one gulp and stared blindly at the far wall. He kept repeating silently, *Don't look into her eyes. Don't look into her eyes.*

Riki couldn't look away from Jason. He was gorgeous. And he was trying so hard not to pressure her. He was adorable, considerate, breathtakingly handsome, and come morning she would know him totally.

The decision was made. All she had to do was say four simple words, make love to me. Now how hard could that be? She was a grown woman with an extensive vocabulary. *Say it, old gal. Say those sweet, blessed four words to end the torment.*

"Jason." Her voice was barely above a whisper.

Jason's jaw clenched together. His knuckles turned white from the grip he had on the arm of the chair. Still he didn't take his gaze off that wall. He knew that if he turned and looked at her, he wouldn't be able to stop. He'd throw her on the floor, with or without her consent. This was too important to them both. What if he misjudged? What if he was reading the message in her eyes wrong? Lord, not another cold shower.

"What?" he asked. His voice was harsh, due to thoughts of cold showers and sleepless nights.

Riki jumped at least two feet off her chair. Her mouth opened but no sound emerged. What went wrong? she wondered frantically. Why was he angry with her? Couldn't he tell that she wanted to make love, couldn't he see it in her eyes? He always seemed to read her soul when he looked into her eyes. Why not now when she needed him to? *Please, oh please, mouth, work. Say those words.* If only Jason would look at her, it would be so much easier. Why was he staring at that wall like he wanted to commit murder? Why wouldn't he at least turn around?

Riki knew she couldn't say those words. Not that she didn't want to. She wanted Jason more than anything in the world. She could feel her breasts swelling with need. Her stomach did a full gainer with a half twist and liquid fire started to burn between her thighs. Her breathing became rapid and shallow, and still the words didn't come.

Her mind was screaming the words, but he wouldn't look at her. She couldn't say them without his help.

Impasse.

Riki old gal, the ball is in your court. Don't blow your foul shot. Do something. If you can't say it, show him.

She took note of his stiff back and the lines on his face. He looked like a marble statue. The beating of his pulse and the flaring of his nostrils were the only signs that he was indeed flesh and bones. What would he do if she threw herself on him? Probably wring her neck by the looks of things. He'd been waiting for her to say she wanted him, and she couldn't. He had every right to wring her neck. He had the right— That was it. She'd write it.

At Riki's sudden movement, Jason stiffened more, waiting for something, anything. What he was not waiting for was Riki scrambling to her desk to write something down. Write something down? Good lord, what in the hell was she doing? Didn't she know what was going on here? Couldn't she feel it? He was going out of his mind.

She turned and hesitantly walked over to him. Her hand was shaking as she held out the piece of paper to him. He took the note and glanced up at her. Her eyes were squeezed tightly shut. He looked at the note clutched in his hand and his heart stopped beating. There in the worst possible handwriting were four simple words. "Make Love to Me."

His head shot up and he grinned with relief and delight. Riki's eyes were still shut. He stood and walked over to the door.

Hearing Jason's movements Riki opened her eyes and turned deadly pale. He was leaving. He was walking out the door. Why didn't the floor open up and swallow her? Why didn't a tornado take her to the Land of Oz? Where in the hell was Auntie Em when you needed her?

He stopped in the doorway and slid the sliding

doors closed. When she heard the click of the lock, she took her first breath since handing Jason the note.

Jason turned around, crossed his arms over his chest, and leaned against the doors. His casual stance was a fake. He was so wound up he was ready to explode, but dammit, he wanted to hear her say it. "Riki, say it." His voice was low and husky.

She took one look at the man she loved and whispered, "Please make love to me."

Neither could say who moved first, but in the next instant Riki found herself in Jason's arms. The kiss started sweet and gentle, totally in conflict with the fierce embrace Jason held her in. Her arms instinctively encircled his neck, and she pressed her breasts against his chest.

At the feel of her unconfined breasts Jason's control snapped. His tongue thrust past her lips to nestle deep within her mouth, to lay claim to what was his. A small moan escaped her throat as her hips met the heat of Jason's desire. His arms tightened to crush her breasts against him, until he could feel the hardened nipples through the layers of clothes that kept them apart. Then he slid one hand down to cup her buttocks and pull her closer to his aroused manhood.

It heightened her desire knowing that he wanted her as much as she wanted him, and heaven knew how much she wanted him. She had never wanted anything more. She had dreamed of Jason, but none of her dreams lived up to the real thing. How could one body hold so much need, so much wanting, so much desire?

She moaned as Jason released her lips to string

a row of kisses to her ear. "Oh, Riki, my love, how I waited for those words." He growled as his mouth slid down her neck, nibbling gently. His hand slipped around her hip, over her stomach, and up to cup her breast. She arched her back and pressed herself into his palm. Her head fell back, and her knees would have given out had he not been holding her.

Jason lowered his head at the invitation and sucked the hard nub through the silk blouse. A jolt went through her as his teeth pulled the nipple farther into his mouth. His name escaped her lips in a pleading, "Jason."

He slowly raised his head to look at her face, to see if her reaction was anything like his. He saw her swollen red mouth and her flushed cheeks, but what really caught his attention was her eyes. Then were half closed with desire, and a flame was burning so brightly in them, it was almost out of control. The desire and passion he could identify, but there was another emotion lying just below the surface. It was there one moment and then gone the next.

He lowered her to the carpet and tenderly kissed her forehead. Rocking back on his heels, he quickly discarded his shirt. "Darlin', I need to feel you touching me."

Her hands went straight to his chest, running through the dark hair. She found his nipples, and at his sharp intake of breath a smile of female satisfaction lit up her face. He saw the smile and growled. "Yes, sir, darlin', you have me hotter than a firecracker on the Fourth of July, but turnabout is fair play."

He swiftly undid all the buttons of her blouse.

Her breath caught at his little-boy smile. A woman could fall in love with that smile, she thought. A woman would do anything to please that "little" boy.

But would she please him? Going through three pregnancies, especially one set of twins, could play hell on a woman's body. Riki knew her weight was good, but no amount of sit-ups would ever firm up the stomach. It still had a soft, rounded look to it. The stretch marks worried her the most. Granted, they had faded with time, but she could still detect the white lines. Jason had never seen his ex-wife when she was pregnant with Charlie. He'd have no idea what carrying a baby for nine months could do. No one had seen her body since Brad, and it was his children that had brought about the changes, so there wasn't too much he could say.

As though he were unwrapping a fragile gift, Jason slowly opened her blouse. His whole attention was on how the silk clung to her damp breast. With a trembling finger, he outlined one nipple, then the other. He raised his eyes to her. "They're beautiful, darlin'."

Riki didn't realize she'd been holding her breath until she let it out. She wrapped her arms around Jason's neck and drew him toward her. "So are you, Jason."

"Beautiful?" At her nod, he chuckled. "Riki, darlin', men are not beautiful."

"Yes, you are. You are also intelligent, sensitive, caring, and sexy."

Jason had to swallow the lump in his throat. Damn, she said the sweetest things. "Ah! Sexy. Now that I can relate to." He placed loud smacking kisses on her neck, and she giggled. "Say 'Uncle' and I'll stop using my wicked charms that are guaranteed to drive women crazy."

She arched her back to rub her breasts across his chest. At the stiffening of his body, she gently bit his ear. "I think crazy is the appropriate word here." Her tongue came out to soothe the area she had just bitten. Feeling him tremble, she did it again.

He drew in a sudden breath. "I think sexy is the appropriate word." His mouth locked with hers and his tongue plunged inside. Her arms tightened around his neck as she gently sucked on his tongue and raised her hips to meet the hard demand of his.

A groan escaped his throat as he broke the kiss. His lips moved to find the sensitive spot behind her ear. "Are you protected?"

As his warm tongue passed over the pulse in her throat, a shiver slid down her back. Protected? No, her heart wasn't protected. It was definitely going to end up in a million pieces when Jason left. His tongue circled her nipple, then he sucked it into his mouth. No, her heart was not protected, and neither was her body. She had never felt anything like this, so this was ecstasy. His lips pressed a kiss in the valley between her breasts, then slowly slipped over to the other nipple.

No, if she were protected an alarm would be ringing right now. Why this man? Why Jason? He was only in her life for a short time. Was ecstasy only hers for such a little while? When Jason left, he would not only take the ecstasy, he'd take her heart.

His tongue circled and then dipped into her navel as he unsnapped her jeans. Protected? Good lord! What had she been thinking? Of course she wasn't protected. It had never entered her mind to think about birth control.

As Riki's warm soft body froze in his arms, Jason raised his head. His eyebrows rose in question. "Riki?"

She couldn't meet his eyes, so she stared at the ceiling. "Uhhh, you're going to have to use something. I'm not protected." Her face changed from the delicate pink of desire to the beet red of embarrassment.

Jason stiffened. She wasn't protected. He was supposed to use something. Hell, he'd come to Virginia to get his daughter. He hadn't come prepared for this. He should have thought of that. Hell, he'd been thinking of nothing but making love to Riki all week. Why hadn't he thought of that?

He looked at the woman lying beneath him, and saw the flush that started at her breast and rose to the top of her head. Taking a deep breath, he dropped a last kiss at the edge of the lace on her bikini underwear. Then, incredibly, he refastened her jeans and shifted his weight off her. He gently cupped her chin and forced her to meet his gaze. He was shocked to see unshed tears swimming in her eyes. He kissed the corner of her mouth. "Why the tears, darlin'?"

"Why aren't you mad?"

"Mad?"

"I'm no expert on the subject," she said, her voice unsteady, "but aren't you supposed to be mad or frustrated or something?"

"Oh, I'm definitely something. And I'm frustrated and mad at myself. I forgot my Boy Scout motto, 'always be prepared.' " There was such a comical leer on his face, she had to chuckle. "That's better." His finger traced the smile on her lips. "But the something I'm feeling is love. I'm falling in love with you, Erika."

She studied his serious face and could only detect honesty in that last statement. Her heart lifted. A soft, gentle understanding shone in her eyes as she replied, "Then I'm the luckiest woman in the whole world."

"Luckiest?"

She reached up and feathered kisses down his throat. "Yes, because I know I'm in love with you, Jason." She tilted her head back and their eyes met. In that instant Riki knew what it was like to look into someone's soul. She also knew what it was like to let someone see into hers.

The kiss they shared was sweet and gentle; it contained all the promises of tomorrow. The seed of love was planted. Now it needed time to grow. Jason's hands slid over her silky smooth back and his embrace tightened. "Ah, Riki darlin', I don't mean to be a party pooper, but if you don't put your blouse back on, I won't be held accountable for my actions."

Her fingers trembled as she tried to button the blouse as fast as possible. Jason noticed the blush on her cheeks and gathered her close. He leaned his back against the desk and positioned her in his lap.

Riki buried her face in his neck. Inhaling the aroma of his after-shave, she gently nipped at his neck. He trembled, and her fingers wandered from his shoulder to his chest. All those afternoons of watching him work outside without a shirt on hadn't prepared her for the feel of his chest. She noticed the width and strength of it, and how smoothly the muscles moved with each movement he made. But she hadn't noticed its warmth, nor the softness of the dark hair that lightly covered it.

She saw his stomach muscles tighten as her fingers trailed down to circle his navel. She'd never thought men's navels erotic. For that matter, men's navels weren't in the top ten things she thought about when thinking of men. Wasn't it amazing what she'd been missing until Jason came along?

His hand shot out and grabbed her wrist, and he gently lifted her hand to his shoulder. "Sorry, darlin', but that isn't a good idea right about now."

She groaned and buried her face in his neck again. How could she be so insensitive? She had never been a tease in her entire life. Tonight certainly was a night for firsts. "Oh, Jason, I'm sorry."

At the sound of remorse in her voice, he tried to lighten the mood. "That's okay, darlin'. But if those fingers traveled any lower, we would have been heading for the kitchen to find some Saran Wrap."

"Saran Wrap?"

"Necessity is the mother of invention."

It took her a few seconds to figure out what Jason meant. She was laughing so hard, she barely managed to ask him if it worked. At his negative response, she was fiercely disappointed.

Her laughing fit was over and the room was silent. The only sound was their light breathing.

One of Jason's arms encircled her, holding her close with his hand resting directly below her breast. The other hand was running through her hair, trying to work out the tangles.

"Darlin', uhh . . . is there a drugstore in town?" His voice had that little boy quality.

She couldn't contain the bubble of laughter that burst from her. "Yes, Jason, our town has a very fine drugstore. I have never seen that certain item you seem to be interested in, though." She raised her head from its resting place on his shoulder to get a good look at him. The red staining his cheeks was enough to start the giggles again. She reached up and ran her finger across his cheek to his lips. His mouth opened and he seductively sucked on her finger.

Her gaze was glued to his mouth as if it were the most fascinating thing she'd ever seen. As his tongue licked the tip of her finger, she lifted her eyes to his. Amusement glinted in them. Ahh, she thought. Punishment for laughing at his blushing. Well, two can play at that. "I can just picture you walking into the drugstore and asking old man Davis for some. I wonder who will turn a brighter red, you or him?"

Jason's eyes lost the amusing glint and started to look dangerous. A wiser woman would have quit while she was ahead, but Riki never had learned the strategy of retreat. "Just think, Jason. If you are real lucky, he'll take you behind the counter and give you a lecture on the evils of the big bad city women."

One moment she was teasing Jason, the next she was flat on her back with her arms pinned above her head. Most of his weight had to be on his knees, she figured, because it wasn't on her hips, which he was straddling. The light of victory shone in his eyes. "Riki, tell me the evils of the big bad city women. This has to be better than that bedtime story you read to Andrew and Billy-Jo tonight."

She was laughing when a thought occurred to her. Jason couldn't possibly walk into Davis's Pharmacy and buy what he wanted. Everyone in town would know what was going on and with whom. There was already speculation on why Jason was visiting. She wouldn't be surprised if everyone was waiting for wedding invitations. She didn't particularly care what people thought of her. She was a grown woman who could make her own decisions. It was Jake and Pete she was concerned about. What if the story got started and somehow wound up affecting the adoption procedures?

Jason saw the serious expression on her face and knew something was wrong. "Riki?"

"You can't go into town and buy them."

"I can't?"

"No. Everyone in town will know what we are doing." Her eyes begged for understanding.

He traced her lower lip with one finger and tried to reassure her. "Okay, darlin', if it bothers you that much what people think, I'll go to a different town tomorrow and see what I can come up with."

She caught hold of his wrist and tried for a better understanding. "Jason, I don't care what people think of me. Believe me, I'll be the luckiest woman in town to have you for a lover. I'm sure some women would turn green with jealousy. It's Jake and Pete I'm worried about. They're not mine yet. I'm not sure if being wanton would count against me." Her teasing smile assured him she wasn't taking it personally.

He let his finger trail down her throat, only to stop when it ran into a barrier of emerald silk. "Are you feeling wanton?"

The only response he received was a groan. He couldn't seem to stop the impulse to kiss her one last time. It was even harder to pull back, knowing that if he continued there would be no stopping for either of them.

As he raised his head and saw the look in her eyes, he told himself he had to get out, while he still could. He stood, then reached down to help her to her feet. He brushed a lock of hair out of her eye and kissed her chastely on her forehead. "I don't want to leave, but if I stay you know what will happen." At her nod, he continued, "I'll take care of our little problem tomorrow."

"Thank you."

"For what?"

She smiled and she brushed her lips across his cheek. "For being Jason."

A whimsical smile was his answer as he turned and walked out the door.

Seven

Three hours and a bleeding arm later, Jason muttered an explicit curse as to what could be done to maple trees. After driving practically to Richmond to find a drugstore open at this time of night, he was in a reckless mood. Maybe he was getting giddy from the lack of sleep, but this had seemed like a good idea when standing on the lawn looking up at Riki's open bedroom window.

The image of Errol Flynn climbing a tree to sneak into his lady's boudoir was romantic. Jason Nesbit stuck in a maple tree with a gash on his arm that probably would require half a dozen stitches just didn't inspire the same feeling. He'd be lucky if Riki hadn't already called the police to report a Peeping Tom.

He sighed with relief when he silently raised the screen and didn't detect any movement from within. Holding his injured arm close to his shirt, hoping not to drip blood all over the place, he slipped over the windowsill. Standing still he could just barely make out Riki's sleeping form nestled on the bed. As he crossed the room he prayed she wouldn't wake up screaming. Gingerly sitting on the edge of the mattress, he whispered her name. The only response he received was an incoherent mumble as she snuggled deeper beneath the quilt.

For the fourth time in the past twenty minutes, doubts assaulted his brain. Maybe he should turn around and climb back down the tree before she woke up. Don Juan he wasn't. The only thing that stopped him from going back over the window ledge was knowing he'd probably fall and break his neck. His arm was hurting like hell, and he wished there was enough light to see what damage had been done.

With his good arm he gently shook her shoulder. He was ready to silence any scream that might be forthcoming, but when she slowly opened her eyes, the only thing forthcoming was a seductive smile.

Riki wasn't sure if she was dreaming or not, but she wasn't going to fight it either way. She'd fallen asleep with fantasies of Jason in her bed, and now that he was here, she wasn't going to let this golden opportunity slip by.

When she reached for him, Jason didn't know if he should laugh at her eagerness or be worried that she didn't seem too upset about a man in her bedroom. "Riki darlin', are you awake?"

As her arms circled his neck she mumbled, "Shh! If I'm not, don't wake me now."

Her lips settled on his. The kiss started out slowly with the promise of things to come. When Riki pressed herself against him to deepen the kiss, the sound of Jason's grunt of pain brought her to awareness. She jerked back to try to focus on him in the darkness.

Not satisfied with the blur in front of her, she reached for the lamp on the nightstand. Momentarily blinded by the sudden light, she missed Jason turning away to hide his arm. As her eyes adjusted, she caught the sheepish grin on his face. After a brief glance at the clock on the nightstand to confirm her suspicion that it was still the middle of the night, the most intelligent thing she could come up with was, "Hi."

"Hi, yourself." He took in her tousled hair, sleep-laden eyes, and the same oversized football jersey he had caught her in the first morning. He was never more aroused by the sight of a woman than he was at that very moment. He reached out and stroked her cheek. "I took care of our problem."

As she caught the spark of desire in his eyes, a soft, inviting smile formed on her lips. "Did you now?"

Jason couldn't believe his luck. She wasn't going to call him names, which he rightly deserved. With the flare of a magician pulling a rabbit out of his hat, he produced a brown bag. At her raised brows, he flashed his little-boy smile and dumped the contents of the bag in her lap.

Riki looked down at six dozen prominent members of the birth control society and mumbled the first thing that came to mind. "Feeling frisky?"

When Jason made a grab to capture her, she noticed the blood on his arm. Her eyes wide with horror, she screeched, "You're bleeding!"

He chuckled. With a curious glance down to confirm that the bleeding had almost stopped, he muttered, "It's only a scratch."

As Riki jumped out of bed grumbling about macho men, he drank in the sight of soft creamy legs that seemed to go on forever. Then he groaned when he caught sight of her cute little tush barely covered by the jersey.

"Are you in pain?" she asked, concerned.

He swallowed, trying to clear his throat, and decided it was safer to nod than to explain exactly where the pain was.

Tugging on his good hand, she practically dragged him into the bathroom. As she flipped the bathroom light on, she ordered, "Take that shirt off." From the medicine cabinet she pulled down disinfectant, gauze, first-aid cream, three different boxes of Band-Aids, scissors, iodine, and medical adhesive tape. Jason began to have second thoughts.

He sat on the closed lid of the commode and held his arm over the sink. "Do you know what you're doing?" he asked.

She gave an indignant huff and stated the obvious. "I am a mother, you know."

Deciding it was safer to change the subject while he was at the mercy of a frustrated Florence Nightingale, he gestured toward her jersey and asked, "Do you always sleep in that?"

Riki wasn't pleased at being caught in an old football shirt that by no stretch of anyone's imagination could be called sexy. So she fluttered her eyelashes and purred, "Only when I'm cold." At Jason's intake of breath, she poured half a bottle of peroxide over the cut.

He half rose off his seat. "Damn, that hurt!" he bellowed.

"Sorry. I'm only trying to kill the germs." Examining the gash for any objects that might be in it, she noticed that the bleeding had almost stopped. She applied pressure to the area with a gauze pad and tuned out Jason's mumbling about sadistic mothers. After making sure the cut had stopped bleeding entirely and was clean, she applied a thin layer of first-aid cream.

Jason stopped her before she could rip into another gauze pad. "It's fine the way it is. Thank you very much, Riki."

She noticed the husky tone in his voice and knew it wasn't caused by pain. His eyes burned into her. Her breathing became shallow and rapid. How could she become so aroused by a simple thank-you? The man practically bled to death in her bathroom and she stood there having sexual fantasies about him. *Morbid, real morbid, Riki.* She took a deep breath to calm her racing heart. "You really should have a bandage on that." At the negative shake of his head, she whispered, "Please."

Jason knew he was a goner. That "please" had come out in the same tone of voice as the "maple syrup" this morning. Desire shot through his body, blood started to heat in his veins, all because of her voice. If she had asked for the moon, he would have gotten it for her. What was a simple bandage? When he saw all the paraphernalia that covered the vanity, he revised his thinking. "Maybe a Band-Aid."

With trembling fingers, she reached for the box with the biggest band-aids in it. Jason's gaze never left her mouth. He was fascinated by the way she sank her teeth into her lower lip when she concentrated. When she raised her eyes and whispered, "All done," his heart skipped a couple of beats. It seemed right when he glanced at his injured arm to see five Band-Aids covering the cut, each with a smiling blue Smurf face on it.

Turning around on the pretense of putting the array of medical supplies away, Riki tried to hide the effect Jason was having on her. How could she be so aroused by him while bandaging his arm? Maybe she was a sadist after all. Deciding a change of thoughts was required, she asked Jason to hand her his shirt.

"No."

Startled by the negative response, she asked, "What do you mean, no? The blood will stain the shirt if it's not soaked right away."

"I don't need a Suzy Homemaker right now."

"Oh."

His voice lowered another notch. "I don't need a Florence Nightingale either."

She watched him rise and take a step toward her. "What do you need, Mr. Nesbit?"

His hand circled the back of her neck and he slowly pulled her toward him. "Erika McCormick, the woman."

Jason meant to go slowly. He really did. But when he felt Riki's hand run down his chest, he lost control. Her fingers tangled in his hair, dark as coal and soft as velvet, as they journeyed to his belt. When she released the buckle, he drew her jersey up over her head.

Seeing her standing there in nothing but a pair of lacy peach-colored panties sent desire sweeping through him like a forest fire. Every nerve ending was attuned to her as he reached to embrace her.

Her luscious breasts crushed against his chest,

rousing a deep groan from the back of his throat. Lifting her so that she was cradled in his arms, he brought his mouth down on hers. He didn't lift his mouth until he had laid her on the tangle of lavender sheets. Lowering his gaze to the lacy peach panties, he gently removed them.

When he stepped back, he couldn't seem to stop trembling. Lifting one foot to remove his sneaker, he noticed Riki's unwavering stare. After shedding his sneakers and socks, he slowly lowered the zipper of his jeans.

He'd never known that green eyes could smolder, but Riki's were smoldering. Sweeping his jeans and briefs off in the same movement, he heard her sharply draw in a breath.

Moving over to make room for Jason, Riki pushed his latest purchases on the floor. Never had she seen such blatant arousal, such strength. They had shared nothing more than a few kisses. Granted, they had melted her socks, but obviously they hadn't melted anything of Jason's. As he stood there, she raised her hand to invite him to her bed.

Seeing Riki reach out to him made Jason smile with satisfaction. She wanted him as much as he wanted her. Lying down next to his emerald-eyed vixen, he drew her into his arms.

Jason dropped small kisses on her forehead, nose, and eyelids, frustrating Riki. Small light kisses were fine at their proper time and place, but this wasn't it. Whispering a husky, "Please," she cupped his face and forced him to meet her waiting lips. Her lips were soft and yielding beneath his demanding ones. As his tongue thrust into her mouth, she rose to meet the challenge and arched her back.

Feeling the neglected, pouting nipples brushing his chest, Jason released her mouth to blaze a trail downward. He captured one of those protruding nubs between his teeth and nipped gently. Riki pulled his head closer, confirming his suspicion that they were on the same wavelength, and slow and easy went flying out the window.

While paying homage to her breast, he slid his hand down over her silky abdomen. It smoothed over her hip to linger on creamy thighs. Then slowly, persistently, his fingers climbed up the inside of her thigh to seek their destiny.

Finding her warm and wet to his touch, Jason suppressed the primitive urge to bang his fists on his chest. As his fingers slid deeper into her moist haven, her hips moved in a rhythm as old as time. When he withdrew to prepare himself, he felt more than heard her frustration. Moving back to settle between her quivering thighs, he murmured, "Riki?"

She gazed at him with passion-filled eyes. "Yes," she whispered as her hips rose to complete the union. Jason entered her in one deep thrust. He clamped his jaw together to control his desire while her body relaxed to accept him. Her deep moan brought an answering one of his own.

With her nails sinking into his shoulders and the heels of her dainty feet digging into the back of his thighs, he started to move his hips. With every thrust he was met equally by the passionate woman beneath him. He could feel the strain in her. She was reaching, stretching, racing toward something she didn't understand. He quickened the pace while whispering against her ivory breasts, "That's it, darlin'. Reach."

The rhythm became frantic, and he had to keep reminding himself to breathe. Sweat broke out of every pore as he took a rosy nipple deep within his mouth, matching the sucking motions to the natural dance of their bodies. Nails dug deeper into shoulders, heels applied bruising pressure, while little animal sounds were murmured with every release of her breath. Her eyes shot open and locked with his. He read amazement, ecstasy, love, and uncertainty in those glistening emerald eyes. He slipped one arm beneath her driving hips to bring her closer. "Let go, darlin'. I've got you. I won't let you go. You're safe."

Trust was the last emotion he read in those eyes before she closed them and cried his name. Hearing that hoarse cry of release, he gave one final thrust and loosed his passion deep within her.

After his breathing slowed to a near-normal rate, he dragged his body off her and cradled her in his arms. Tenderly he brushed back a lock of auburn hair that clung to her face. Her eyes slowly opened to reveal contentment as a slow, wondrous smile curved her mouth. He lowered his head to kiss the tip of her nose. "That was perfect, Erika," he murmured.

How could anything be so perfect? she wondered. She had never felt anything like that before in her life. Good Lord, was that normal? Was it supposed to be like that all the time? If that happened every time with Jason, she'd be dead by thirty-five. Considering she was thirty, that left her five good years. What a way to go! With a satisfied smile, her only comment before she fell asleep was, "And you only used one hand."

It was still dark when Riki woke to the feel of a warm hand sliding up her thigh. Jason. Snuggling her tush against his obvious arousal, she smiled with anticipation. How could he possibly want her again? Was this normal? The hell with being normal. This was way more fun.

Feeling Riki wiggle against him, Jason growled. He nibbled on the back of her neck as he slowly slid his hand over her hip, across her stomach, and up to cup her breast. Another growl escaped him when he felt the nipple harden in his palm. What this woman did to him ought to be against the law.

Nothing in his life had prepared him for Riki. The need to protect her and cherish her . . . The compulsive desire to make her smile, along with the absolute necessity to become one with her. This went beyond sex. This was the woman he wanted to wake up with for the rest of his life. Hers was the face he wanted to see across the bowl of Cheerios for the rest of his days.

Hearing her soft purr broke his control. He turned her so she was lying completely beneath him and fully aware of his need. With most of his weight on his injured arm, he released her breast and let his hand slip down over her stomach, past the auburn curls, and sink deep within her.

At her gasp of pleasure he whispered, "Good morning." Then, feeling the warm reception she gave him, he groaned and murmured, "Perfect morning," before his mouth came down on hers.

•   •   •

When the alarm went off Riki pulled the pillow over her head. As the buzzer kept on buzzing she cautiously peeked out from her hiding place to realize she was alone. She shut off the alarm and glanced toward the bathroom. Empty. He had left. Maybe he hadn't even been there. Maybe she'd dreamed it all.

Seeing the slight indentation on the other pillow, she knew she hadn't dreamed it. So where was he? A frown was just settling on her brow when she noticed a note propped against her dresser mirror. She smiled as she pulled the discarded jersey over her head, then padded barefoot to the dresser.

A silly grin broke out as she read the note. "Perfect morning to you, my love. Thought I'd leave before the Munchkins appeared. It would be kind of difficult to explain our pajama party—since we didn't have any pajamas on." At the bottom was a large "J."

Standing barefoot in the kitchen and staring at the gooey mess in the frying pan, Riki wondered what she was supposed to be cooking. She was pretty sure it was going to be scrambled eggs, but it didn't look like any scrambled eggs she had ever seen. What in the world did she put in it? She decided it was safer to dump it all and start over.

Jason stood in the kitchen doorway and studied the woman scraping the frying pan and singing a Willie Nelson tune. Starting at pink toenails and traveling up faded skin-tight blue jeans to an old Betty Boop T-shirt, and topped with a bouncing auburn pony tail, she was gorgeous. And she was his.

Pulling his gaze away from that luscious body

before he embarrassed himself, he noticed for the first time the chaos of the kitchen. Lunch boxes were spread across the counters in total disorder. Laundry was thrown in piles on the floor. The coffee maker was still dripping, only someone had forgotten to add the coffee grounds. A box of corn-flakes had spilled under the table and Tiny was cleaning up the mess.

All the kids were shouting and arguing with one another. Poor Billy-Jo was sitting at the table wearing a shirt, no pants, and one sock. She was blissfully unaware that her mother had only put half her hair in a pigtail, and it looked like she was eating chocolate chip cookies for breakfast. Jake had just finished pouring orange juice in his bowl of Fruit Loops. When he proceeded to eat them without the slightest hesitation, a shudder slid down Jason's back.

Travis and Trevor were arguing over a baseball card. Meanwhile Andrew lifted his cereal bowl and slurped the remaining milk. Pete was trying to unscrew the back of his hearing device with a butter knife. The only person halfway normal was Charlie. She sat there eating Cheerios as if nothing were out of the ordinary. She was dressed for school, except Riki hadn't braided her hair yet. When Charlie caught sight of Jason standing there, she gave him a tentative smile. He smiled back.

Travis noticed Jason and shouted, "Hi, Jason." That was immediately followed by a chorus of hi's. After greeting all the Munchkins he purposely walked to Riki.

When she heard all the children greeting Jason, Riki had turned from the stove. She watched him saunter across the room to her. He was wearing paint-splattered sneakers, worn and faded jeans, and a blue T-shirt that proclaimed a Fiddlers' Convention in Austin, Texas, and he was gorgeous. She felt her heart rate increase. How did he do that just by walking across the room? When her glance lifted to his face, the noise in the room shifted into the background. Aware only of silver eyes that could speak a thousand words, she read warmth, desire, possession, and the shiny light of love in them. When he stopped a few inches from her, she smiled shyly and whispered what she thought appropriate for the situation. "Good morning."

"No, darlin', it's a perfect morning." Stroking her lower lip with a rough finger tip he said, "I love you, Erika." She watched in wonderment while he lowered his head until their lips met in a sweet, soul-shaking kiss.

Her arms were encircling his neck when the sound of children penetrated her desire-fogged mind. "Yuck, that's gross," Travis said.

"What's gross?" Jake asked, his head tilted, trying to hear some sound.

"Jason's kissing Mom." Trevor shuddered. "Ugh! Who would kiss a girl?"

"Maybe she has a boo-boo," Andrew said.

Quickly backing up to put some distance between herself and Jason, Riki knew her face was beet red. Why hadn't she thought of the kids before she kissed him? Because she never could think straight when Jason was in the same room. He pulled her back to him, and she buried her face in his chest. With her cheek pressed against him, she could hear the rhythmic beating of his heart and his jerky breathing. That could mean one of two things. Either Jason was very aroused or he was trying desperately not to laugh. Considering he was holding her tightly against him and she could feel every one of his muscles, that left out physical arousal. So he thought it was funny, did he? Well, if it weren't so embarrassing being caught in a clinch over the cornflakes by seven rug rats, she might be inclined to laugh herself.

Hearing the kids discussing the grotesqueness of kissing was just too much. Humor won out. Burying her face deeper into Jason's collarbone to try to suppress the laughter, she smelled the clean, fresh aroma of him—a combination of soap, shaving cream, and the musk scent that was uniquely his. She tried to pull her thoughts away from Jason before she did something really embarrassing—like ripping off his shirt so she could trace that marvelous collarbone with her tongue. It finally occurred to her that the Munchkins were still debating the merits of kissing.

"Did you see how he kissed her before breakfast?" Travis said knowingly. "That's so he doesn't upchuck his breakfast."

"Do they really throw up after kissing?" Jake asked.

"They don't throw up on TV," Trevor said.

"Who threw out the TV?" Pete shouted.

"Put your hearing aid back in, Pete."

"They don't throw up," Trevor stated.

"Do so."

"Do not."

"Yeah, well, if I had to kiss a girl, I would," Travis insisted. "Yuck!"

Jason tilted up Riki's face with the tip of one

finger under her chin. Smiling, he said, "It seems you are neglecting the boys' education."

"Don't you think they're too young?"

"Maybe for some things, but to think you can get sick by kissing a girl is a little drastic, isn't it?" Maybe it wasn't, he thought. How was he to know? He was new at this parenthood number. It was a lot tougher than he'd originally figured.

"They're just not used to seeing their mother kissed in the kitchen by a strange man."

"Am I?"

"Are you what?"

"Strange." He watched the various expressions chase one another across Riki's face. When the mischievous gleam appeared in her eyes, he knew he was in trouble.

"No, you're not strange." She raised herself upon her toes to whisper in his ear. "But if last night you had wanted to . . ." As Jason's jaw dropped open and his arms fell limply to his sides, his eyes registered shock, bewilderment, and a touch of sexual awareness. She gently raised his chin until his mouth was closed and with a twinkle in her eye announced, "Now that's strange."

Forcing her attention on the children, she noticed for the first time the chaotic mess. Mentally lecturing herself on daydreaming in the middle of the morning, she casually lifted an empty bowl off Billy-Jo's head. Issuing orders to the children that would have done a drill sergeant proud, she hurriedly finished packing lunches. When Billy-Jo started to chant "potty, potty," she told Jason to brush Charlie's hair while she handled Billy-Jo.

Returning to the kitchen with a dressed Billy-Jo in tow, she couldn't help but smile at the picture of all the older children lined up, complete with backpacks and lunch pails. At the end of the line was Charlie with a lopsided ponytail and a huge grin.

Kissing everyone's cheeks as they filed out the back door, she couldn't help but think how Jason fit into the family perfectly. She couldn't squelch the image of him actually living with them. The tantalizing thoughts of being married to Jason and keeping Charlie, whom she had come to love like a daughter, were firmly placed in her brain.

Ideas on how to persuade Jason to give up a whole company and settle in the hills of Virginia to raise seven children chased one another around in circles as she cleaned the kitchen. He was attracted to her, and he had proclaimed his love, but was that enough? Charlie accepted him as part of the family, so there really was no reason to keep Charlie in Virginia. Besides that, it wasn't fair to use his own daughter against him, was it? Something still didn't seem right there. With everything Riki knew about her, Charlie should not have reacted so positively toward Jason.

While loading the dishwasher, she decided she really couldn't hold him here against his will, but she'd try to entice that will. She was going to shower him with so much love, he wouldn't want to go back to Dallas. And if the day came when he and Charlie walked out that door, she'd throw the biggest thing she could find at his fat head.

After putting the first load of wash into the machine, she started to scrape the frying pan again. She was singing along with the radio when she was grabbed from behind and lifted into the air.

She let out a squeal as Jason's warm lips started nibbling on the back of her neck. The squeal died into a moan as he set her on her feet. His strong hands left her waist to cup her breasts. A shiver slid down her back as he lovingly bit her earlobe. Her voice held a silent plea for more as she asked, "What are you doing?"

Feeling Riki's nipples harden sent a shaft of heat through Jason's loins. Trying to strive for some lightness before he made a total fool of himself, he mumbled, "Having breakfast. I seem to have missed out this morning, and a man can't survive by love alone." He added silently that he was willing to try.

He chuckled when she glared at the frying pan hanging limply in her hand and muttered something about men's stomachs. It was quite obvious she had her mind on something other than cooking. For that matter, so did he. But short of locking two small children in a closet, there wasn't a whole lot they could do about it. He gently turned her in his arms and held her tight, resting his chin on top of her head. Running his hands down her spine to her hips, he tucked her closer to him.

When he felt her stiffen as she made contact with his unmistakable arousal, he took a deep breath. "Disgusting what one little old T-ball coach can do to a man's libido, isn't it?" Feeling her wiggle her hips to get closer called for more self control than he thought he was capable of. Holding her hips still and trying to put a few desperately needed inches between them proved to be a task worthy of Hercules. "Erika, Billy-Jo and Andrew are in the house. And if you don't stop that wiggling they are going to be mighty shocked to see their mother flat on her back on the kitchen table."

Using her free hand she cupped the back of his head to bring his lips closer. "What are they doing?"

Seeing the smoldering desire in her eyes, Jason knew he was going down for the count. "I left them in front of the television watching some big yellow bird."

A slow sensual smile curved her mouth. "That should keep them busy for the best part of an hour." Seeing Jason hesitate, trying to decide if it was worth the risk, she added a little incentive.

A shudder slid down his back as he watched her small pink tongue slide over her lower lip. His mind was screaming, *slow and easy, don't overwhelm her with too much too soon.* His body, though, was howling, *take her, she's asking for it. What are you waiting for, an engraved invitation?*

Realizing that he wasn't going to kiss her, Riki ran her fingers through his thick black hair. Indecision still flickered in his eyes, and she slowly traced the outside of his ear. Lowering her voice an octave, trying for that husky sound that was supposed to drive men crazy, she asked, "What do you want, Jason?"

His mind shouted, *you, now, hard and fast.* Gazing at this woman who promised paradise, he wondered why common sense always showed up at the most inappropriate times. He was a grown man. If he couldn't control his sexual urges for the next twelve hours or so, he was in big trouble. Looking straight into her eyes he replied, "Eggs."

"Eggs?"

"Yeah, eggs, scrambled and with ketchup." Turning on his heels he marched out the kitchen door.

Riki blinked at the empty doorway, wondering what had happened. He was responding to her one minute and the next he ordered eggs. *You're in bad shape, old girl, if he prefers scrambled eggs over you. And with ketchup dumped on top no less. Yuck!*

Scrambling eggs once more, Riki decided that affirmative action was called for. How could she possibly shower Jason with love if he treated her as a waitress? There was an old saying about training a mule. The first thing you did was beat him with a two-by-four across the head—to get his attention. Well, she really didn't want to whack Jason across the head, but she did need to get his attention.

Eight

After being practically ignored during breakfast, Riki started concocting a sketchy plan. While she cleaned up the kitchen for the second time a distinctive mischievous laugh followed her around. Heading upstairs to change from her jeans, she decided the day was going to be a scorcher, in more ways than one.

Digging deep in the back of a dresser drawer she finally found what she had been looking for—a pair of white shorts. She grabbed a lavender tank top and stepped into the bathroom.

It took a deep breath to snap the shorts finally. After slipping into the snug top, she hesitantly glanced in the mirror. Good Lord, talk about second skin. Critically examining her body, she concluded it would pass. It wasn't any great shakes, but Jason hadn't screamed in horror last night.

With the thought of last night lingering in her mind, she remembered a part of her anatomy that seemed to fascinate Jason. Turning around to get a rear view in the full length mirror, she studied that particular article. She decided that it could have been a tiny bit smaller and a lot firmer, but all in all it wasn't bad for a mother of four. She twisted her hair up into a casual knot, took one last look in the mirror, then headed out to conquer the enemy—or at least to seduce him.

Jason nearly had heart failure when he rounded the side of the house and spotted Riki bent over stirring paint. Her back was to him and her provocative derriere swayed as she stirred. He swallowed the growl that was about to emerge from his throat. He lowered his gaze to her feet and leisurely traveled up lightly tanned calves. His pulse quickened. As he stared at the back of satiny knees, he remembered the scent of her perfume that she'd applied there, and he ran his tongue over suddenly dry lips.

Blood was pounding in his temples as his gaze continued up her creamy thighs. How could a relatively small woman have such long legs? Trying to swallow a lump, he fastened his hungry gaze on her gently rounded tush. Didn't she realize that her stirring caused that fabulous part of her body to jiggle, and that it was driving him nuts? How was he going to make it until bedtime if he couldn't even make it to lunch, for cripesake? Visions of those soft creamy thighs wrapped around him were having an adverse effect on his libido. A harsh sound of self-disgust emerged from his throat before he could stop it.

That sound was the confirmation Riki had been waiting for. Despite feeling tingling sensations for the past several minutes, she had continued to stir perfectly mixed paint. Now she swiveled her head but did not straighten. What she saw caused her breath to jam in her chest.

Jason stood there with a clenched jaw and white knuckles, gripping the handles of three paint cans. She let the wooden stirrer slip from her fingers and turned to face the man she loved.

He tore his gaze from hers to glance at Billy-Jo and Andrew, riding their Big Wheels on the porch. She watched helplessly as he then pivoted and marched away, his muttered curse barely reaching her ears.

Taking the first breath of air since she had looked up at him, Riki tried to regain her equilibrium. As she gazed at the two children playing on the porch, her heart swelled with pride and love. For the first time she realized that it wasn't going to be easy to conduct a fiery love affair with seven children around.

Walking slowly toward the porch, she thought about what had just transpired with Jason. She sank down on the steps, her elbows on her knees and her chin cupped in her palms. She came to the conclusion that she wasn't very proud of herself. How could she blatantly tease him like that—especially when there was nothing he could do about it with the children up and around? It looked like she owed that poor man an apology. Now, Miss Smarty, figure out what you're going to say.

She was so deep in thought she didn't notice Jason until he sat down next to her. She had just opened her mouth to apologize when he placed his finger on her lips.

His "I'm sorry" was a mere whisper.

"For what?" Now she was thoroughly baffled.

"For walking away, for losing control, for ignoring you this morning."

"Why?"

Sighing with frustration, he gazed into her eyes and told her the truth. "Because I can't look at you and not want you. I thought it was bad for the last two weeks, wanting you and not having you. But after last night, I have to have more." He raked his hand through his hair. "Can you forgive me?"

"Forgive you! I thought you wanted eggs!"

"Eggs?" Now it was Jason's turn to be baffled.

Glancing over toward the children still playing, she was eternally grateful to the inventor of the Big Wheel. "This morning I asked you what you wanted. You said eggs. Scrambled eggs with ketchup." She shivered to emphasize the revulsion she felt toward ketchup on eggs.

Jason looked at her incredulously. "And you believed that?"

"Why wouldn't I believe that? That's what you said." Trying to keep her voice low yet forceful was a lot harder than she had imagined. Hers came out squeaky and weak.

Seeing Jason struggling not to laugh snapped all her control. "And to think I was going to apologize to you. You can go to—" She glanced around to verify that the children were within hearing distance, even if they weren't overly interested in their conversation. "—to Satan himself before I apologize to you, you big insensitive baboon." She leaped to her feet and started to march off, only to be grabbed from behind and swung up into the air.

It was definitely an unfair tactic, she decided,

to be cradled against a muscular chest. One of Jason's hands supported her back while the other cupped her bare thigh, and his touch chased all thoughts of further arguments from her mind. As he lowered himself back down onto the step, he didn't loosen his grip on her. Gently pushing a few wisps of hair from her face, he said, "Now I know where the red hair comes in."

Riki could feel herself losing ground. She couldn't argue with Jason while sitting on his lap, so she gave a noncommittal answer of "Mmmm."

"I would like to apologize," he continued, "for that little white lie this morning. If I had told you what I really wanted, I would have probably shocked you to death."

Mulling this over, Riki decided some more truth was in order. "I doubt it. You see, I was probably thinking the same thing." Feeling Jason's silent chuckle, she continued. "Now I would like to apologize."

"What for?"

She hid her face in his neck when she felt the flush of embarrassment sweep up her cheeks. "Well," she mumbled, "I kind of took offense at coming in second to scrambled eggs."

"With ketchup, no less."

"Really, it's the ketchup that did it. I don't mind losing fair and square to something white and round, but to lose to something red and runny was more than my pride could stand."

After a long pause, Jason said, "And?"

"Well, I kind of set out to seduce you."

Feeling his finger under her chin she closed her eyes. His lips whispered soft kisses across her closed lids. "Erika, please open your eyes."

Peeking out from beneath thick dark lashes, she was reassured that at least he wasn't angry. When a person sits on another person's lap, she becomes aware of things that ordinarily are missed, like the tightening of his thighs, the hardness growing behind his zipper, and the rapid beating of his heart beneath her hand. Knowing she could rouse this reaction from him without so much as a kiss made desire race through her veins.

"Is that why you are wearing the shortest pair of shorts I have ever seen?"

"Uh-huh."

She felt his groan more than heard it, and smiled. "Does that mean I could seduce you?"

Looking into twinkling green eyes Jason wondered what he was going to do with her. Keep her was the top choice, but making love until she never doubted her attraction again ran a very close second. Chuckling, he replied, "Riki darlin', you could seduce a dead man."

"What would I want with a dead man?" Her husky voice left him in no doubt what she would do with a live one. Almost unbearably excited at the thought of being seduced, he was lowering his mouth to her eagerly awaiting one when someone attached himself to his back.

"Hi, Jason, what are you doing?"

He turned his head and encountered the curious stare of Andrew. "I'm going to kiss your mother."

"Why?"

"Because I like to kiss your mother."

"Can I watch?"

"No."

"Why?"

Feeling Riki silently laughing in his arms, he turned his attention back to her. "You think this is funny?"

"I did warn you about Andrew." She tried to control the laughter, but without much success.

Leaning down to steal a quick hard kiss before the opportunity was completely gone, Jason decided that would have to do until after the kids' bedtime. He stood with Riki still in his arms, then gently lowered her feet to the ground. Stepping back, he motioned to the house. "Don't we have a house to paint?"

She saluted. "Yes, sir."

"Then get busy with those shutters." He affectionately patted her sweet tush, then whistling softly, strolled around the side of the house.

After homework, an early dinner, and T-ball practice, everyone was in dire need of soap and water. With seven children in the house, there was a definite method to the madness. First Billy-Jo and Andrew got a bath, then Charlie took a shower, then the boys took turns in order of first come, first served. One of these years, Riki thought as the twins raced past her, she'd get around to putting that other bath in upstairs.

Snack time seemed to drag. The only highlight was the whipped cream the kids sprayed on their Jell-O. Seeing Jason eyeing the can, she asked, "Do you want some?"

His husky reply left her in no doubt as to what he had in mind. "Can I have mine later?"

Good lord, she thought, did people really do that? She'd heard of things like that, but personally never experienced them. *Come on, old girl, this is supposed to be a lusty love affair. If Jason thinks whipped cream is lusty, go for it.* Smiling slightly, she replied, "Sure, as long as you do the laundry."

Having coffee go down the wrong pipe is not considered socially graceful, but when Riki spoke Jason had a mouthful of coffee. Finally catching his breath he glared at her. She had her hand raised to whack him again on the back, when he managed to get out a choked, "Don't."

"Are you okay?"

He took a deep breath. "Fine." After sending her a questioning glance, he asked, "Do you know what you just agreed to do?"

Pausing to consider the question, she was pretty sure she had the general idea. How many different things could two people do with one can of whipped cream? Vivid images of Jason and herself exploring a couple of possibilities ran through her mind. While not the height of sexual excitement to her, they didn't actually repulse her. If he had any other ideas on the subject, she might as well know now if he was kinky. She just hoped he wouldn't bring out the whips and chains. Laughter bubbled in her throat at the thought of Jason being kinky. Looking him dead in the eyes she said tentatively, "I think so."

Jason decided it was a good thing he hadn't drunk any more coffee, because he would have choked for the second time. Her honesty never failed to amaze him. Was she willing to follow his lead, or was she a secret whipped cream connoisseur? Now that could pose some delightful possibilities, although he had never tried it himself.

Listening to the children's chatter around the table, he decided a change in conversation was in order after one last statement. "I'll keep that in mind for future reference." She smiled with relief, and he felt vaguely disappointed.

For half an hour after tenderly tucking Charlie and the other children into bed, Jason paced nonstop. Riki filled the dishwasher, scrubbed a pan soaking since dinner, and set out lunch boxes for the morning. After she had wiped the kitchen table for the third time, he muttered, "Do you think they're all asleep yet?"

At his hopeful expression, she chuckled. "If they haven't come down by now, there's a good chance they're all sleeping."

She barely had the last word out of her mouth when he swooped her up in his arms and marched out of the room. Taking time only to check the lock on the back door and switch off the lights, he headed for the stairs.

"Not even a courtesy kiss," she complained. "Is this what is known as a 'wham, bam, thank you, ma'am'?"

He stopped on the third step to look down at the precious bundle cradled in his arms. "I'll have you know," he said haughtily, "that I have never 'wham, bammed' in my life." Then his voice dropped an octave. "If I had kissed you before, darlin', we never would have made it to the bedroom."

"Oh?"

"Yes, oh." He proceeded up the stairs and down the hallway.

They were two steps away from the door to

heaven when a voice floated out of the dark hallway. "Hi, Jason, what are you doing?"

Jason stopped dead. Clamping his jaw shut and
staring at the closed door in front of him, he felt
Riki stiffen in his arms. She peered over Jason's
rigid shoulder at her youngest son. "Andrew, what
are you doing up?"

"I was thirsty."

"Go to the bathroom and get yourself a cup of
water."

"Okay." He turned to go, then turned back. "Why
is Jason carrying you?"

Riki was positive she heard Jason mutter a
curse as he slowly lowered her to her feet. "Because I have a splinter in my foot."

"Can I see?"

"No."

"Why?"

This time Jason answered. "I already took it
out. I was just carrying your mother because it's
still tender." He leaned down to whisper in her
ear. "Get ready for bed, and whatever you do,
don't shut your window." At her questioning look
he continued in a normal tone for Andrew's sake,
"Now you go get your drink of water. I'm leaving.
Don't worry, I'll lock up behind me." As she opened
her mouth to protest, he added, " 'Night, Andrew.
I'll see you around, Riki." With a few quick strides
he disappeared down the stairway.

Riki was positive there was a code in there somewhere, but she couldn't find it. She tucked Andrew back into bed after his drink, then slowly
walked down the hall to her room.

She was closing the door and switching on the

light when she was startled to see Jason sitting in the wing chair. "Jason?"

"It's about time you got here," he said as he rose from the chair. He reached her in three strides. Gathering her close he covered her mouth with a kiss so urgent, she responded instinctively.

She pulled his polo shirt over his head as he undid the row of buttons down the front of her blouse. As she threw the shirt over his shoulder, she heard his sudden intake of breath.

"My Lord," he exclaimed, "you're wearing it?"

She was concentrating on unbuckling his belt. "What?"

He removed her hands from the snap of his jeans and slid the blouse from her shoulders. As it fell to the floor he said in a hoarse voice, "The green teddy."

Both snaps on their jeans were undone together. Both zippers were lowered simultaneously. When he impatiently brushed her hands aside, she purred, "Do you like it?"

He nimbly slid her jeans down her silken thighs. "Like is not the verb I would use to describe my feelings for your teddy." He held her while she stepped out of the pants. By the time she was standing in front of him wearing nothing but the teddy and a smile, he was completely naked.

She stopped him before he could lift her in his arms, gesturing toward the door. As his brow rose in question, she whispered, "I've got to lock the door. The boys are at a very impressionable age."

"So am I," he said as the lock clicked. "I'm very impressed." Then he swept her up in his strong arms and carried her to the bed.

• • •

Swatting at the alarm the next morning Riki had to marvel at that man's stamina. She counted her lucky stars that she had met him when he was the ripe age of thirty-six and not twenty-one, when presumably men are at their peak. Flopping back against her pillow, she noticed her bedroom door was standing open and the mischievous mint teddy thrown haphazardly across the notorious brass bed's footrail.

She sank deeper into the warmth of the quilt and chuckled as she remembered Jason's reaction after the first time they made love and he realized the teddy never made it the whole way off. Quickly disrobing her completely, he explained it wasn't proper to make love to a partially clad woman. Then he preceded to make love to her properly. Any more proper and she would have been a dead woman.

Giving herself a mental pep talk, she left the warmth of tangled sheets that smelled of her perfume, his after shave, and the essence of their lovemaking. As she stood under the warm water, she wondered what it would be like to shower with Jason. She glanced down to see the faded stretch marks and immediately canceled that fantasy. Jason had had plenty of opportunity to notice them, since he believed in making love with the lights on. He couldn't have possibly gotten any closer to them, unless he were grafted to her.

Either he didn't care and they didn't bother him, or he had seen other women with them and knew what they were. Well, hers were the only stretch marks he'd see from now on, because as of today Jason Nesbit was off the market. He was unequivocally spoken for. Now how does one tell a man that?

Jason strolled into the kitchen and came to a standstill at the look of determination on Riki's face. All seven children sat at the table neatly dressed and ready for school. The amazing thing was not a word was being spoken. The only sound was the "snap, crackle, pop" of their cereal. Many a man would have turned and run. Jason considered himself either very brave or extremely stupid.

Purposely smiling his famous little-boy smile, he walked over to Riki. She watched him approach, her arms folded over her chest, one foot tapping. It was definitely not a good sign. When she opened her mouth and started, "You, Mr. Nesbit, have absolutely seen your last—" he clamped his hand across her mouth before she could complete the sentence. Telling the children to continue with breakfast, he practically dragged her out the back door.

Stopping when they were far enough away from the house that the children couldn't overhear, he removed his hand. "Okay, darlin', continue."

She took a deep breath and began at the beginning. "You, Mr. Nesbit, have absolutely seen your last stretch mark. I don't share." Having said her final say, she crossed her arms again and dared him to disagree.

Thinking the whole thing through still made no sense to him. He had no idea what she was talking about. "I think I lost something somewhere."

"You, Mr. Nesbit, didn't question my stretch

marks." Let him deny that, she thought, and she'd pop him in his chops.

There was such a thing as social etiquette, Jason mused. A man did not question a lady's stretch marks. Since she'd had four children, he might have questioned the lack of marks. "Was I supposed to?" Maybe there was something special about her stretch marks. Heaven knew he wasn't an expert on the subject, but he had seen them once or twice before.

"Of course not!"

Totally bewildered now, he ran a hand through his hair. "Then what in the hell are you talking about?"

"Commitment."

"I thought we were talking about stretch marks?" he snapped, clearly at the end of his patience.

"That was only here or there."

"Riki darlin', I haven't had my morning cup of coffee yet, so please be aware that I am trying to follow this conversation." At her nod of understanding, he asked, "You want a commitment?"

"Yes."

Sheer joy flooded his body. She wanted a commitment. Here he'd been going slow and easy and she was asking for—no, demanding—a commitment. He took a deep breath and asked the critical question. "What sort of commitment?"

She rubbed a throbbing temple as she thought of how to answer that. She couldn't very well demand marriage. This might be the age of liberated women, but she wasn't that liberated. "As long as you're seeing me, you won't be seeing other women."

"What other women?" he roared.

"The ones with the stretch marks."

"Oh, lord, we're back to them again." He raked his hand through his hair again and was surprised to see it come out empty. He really felt like pulling all his hair out. "Okay, darlin', very slowly, explain that comment."

For the first time Riki questioned her thinking. Right now Jason really didn't seem like the sweet-tempered, loveable man she knew and loved. "Well, when you didn't question my stretch marks I got to thinking either you didn't care or that you were used to seeing them." He nodded for her to continue. "Anyway, I thought how could you not care about them. So that left your seeing someone else with them."

Seeing confusion in her eyes, he gently cupped her shoulders. "Listen, Riki, I am only going to explain this once. I am a full-grown man of thirty-six. I know what stretch marks are. I am not seeing any women with stretch marks, or any other women for that matter, except you. Your marks don't repulse me. In fact, I would have to say the opposite. I'm jealous that it wasn't my babies that gave you them. Now for the commitment part, I have no intentions of seeing other women. You are my lady, end of statement. I happen to be very possessive of what is mine."

"Really?"

"Really." Hauling her bodily into his embrace, he proceeded to kiss her good morning. Breaking the kiss before it became unmanageable, he chuckled. "I knew I was in trouble the moment I spotted your red hair."

"It's not red!"

"Is so."

"It only has red highlights," she mumbled as she stood on tiptoe to kiss his cheek.

"Thank goodness for small favors. I don't think I could handle you with totally red hair." He brushed a soft kiss across her lips. "Did I wish you a perfect morning?"

Returning the feather kiss with one of her own, she answered, "You just did."

"I had better get those kids moving before they miss their bus. It looks like I'm going to have another late breakfast."

He draped his arm across her shoulders and they started back to the house. Right before they entered the kitchen she whispered in his ear how she could possibly make up the late breakfast to him. At his growl she giggled and entered the room full of kids.

Jason was busy ushering kids out the door when Travis—or was it Trevor?—said, "I wish you could kiss Mom more. Maybe she wouldn't be so grumpy in the morning." Laughing out loud, Jason turned to Riki. Seeing her stick her tongue out confirmed she had heard the comment.

Yes, sir, it certainly was a perfect morning.

Nine

After dinner and with everyone dressed in their matching blue T-shirts, they headed for the van. Raw energy and tension crackled in the air. Tonight was their first game. The boys were all giving their expert opinion to one another. Even Jake had a firm belief concerning what should and shouldn't be done.

Jason had never seen anything more vicious than a parent whose son was just called out. He had never been to a Little League ball game before, and to say it was culture shock was an understatement. While Riki's team was at least halfway normal—he counted Mr. Farley parking the hearse at the curb a little extreme—the other team bordered on ridiculous. Not only did they have the matching shirt and cap, they had matching pants and socks. Every boy on the team was wearing spikes and wrist bands, and had a pair of batting gloves hanging out of his back pocket. By the bottom of the second inning it was obvious that fancy uniforms don't make ball players.

Jason was sitting on the bench next to Jake with Billy-Jo on his lap. Charlie and Andrew held their key positions next to the bats. The score was tied three to three. Little Tommy was finally on base, third to be precise. How he had gotten there Jason hadn't a clue. The poor kid had such a limp that no matter how far he hit, he couldn't run the bases fast enough.

Travis was up, there was one out, but the play was at home. Travis hit a high pop to the second baseman, who caught it and threw it home. Jason had to admit Tommy gave it his best shot. He even slid the last ten feet. He was definitely out. Anyone could see that.

As soon as the umpire called the out, Riki went charging in. She didn't stop until she was nose to nose with the two-hundred-and-fifty-pound umpire. Her ponytail was bobbing, her cheeks were flushed, and her arms were gesturing wildly. Everyone in the stands could hear her. She very politely and bluntly was telling the umpire what she thought of his eyesight. At one point she threatened to pull Jake in to ump the rest of the game, because obviously he had better eyesight.

The poor umpire never had a chance. Jason had never seen Riki so infuriated, and was starting to believe Tommy might have been safe. The umpire was a brilliant red at this point, hardly getting in the first syllable of a sentence. Riki raised her fist and waved it under his nose.

The umpire looked ready to pick her up and ditch her in the Dumpster. Jason decided this had gone far enough. No one was going to lay a finger on his Riki. He cautiously set Billy-Jo on the bench and started out to the field.

At that point Riki made a comment only the umpire could hear. If anything he turned redder. She marched back toward the bench with her breast heaving. The light of victory was in her eyes, but Jason couldn't figure out why. The decision remained the same. Cries of "You tell him, Riki" and "Always said he was as blind as a bat" were coming from some of the parents in the stand.

Riki placed a comforting hand on Tommy's shoulder. The little boy smiled and hugged her. As the team gathered up their gloves and headed for the outfield, Riki leaned against the fence and marked her clipboard.

"Hey, coach."

"Yes, Mr. Nesbit?"

"Didn't you know that Tommy was really out?"

"Of course."

He stared at her in total confusion. "Then why did you practically cause World War Three over it?"

"Besides the fact that I'm the only female coach and wanted him to know I won't be pushed?"

"Besides that."

"Because if I did nothing, Tommy would have started to cry. It was the first time he had ever made it to home plate. Now he knows I have confidence in him and it doesn't seem so bad that he was out."

She gazed into Jason's eyes to see if he understood. His expression softened and she knew he did. He leaned forward and kissed her softly.

"Did I tell you today that I love you?"

"Yep. That just made it number three."

"Keeping track?"

"Yep." She started to giggle.

"Why?"

"Because for every time you say it I am going to . . ." She whispered the rest into his ear, then turned back toward the game, shouting, "Let's play ball."

Jason leaned his forehead against the fence. "Why now, lord? Why does she say things like that here?" Taking a few deep breaths to steady himself, he turned back toward the bench.

That night set the pattern for the next two weeks. During the day Riki handled the domestic end of the home, while Jason finished painting. His next projects were to repair the treacherous brick walk to the front door and to somehow speed up the relationship with Riki. He'd been in Virginia for nearly a month now. Charlie seemed to accept him. His brother-in-law Sam was running his business with no major problems. The problems that did crop up were handled with a couple of long-distance calls. For some reason climbing that tree every night was becoming less and less appealing. Not the lovely woman waiting for him every night. She was quickly becoming a necessity. His business couldn't hang forever, though, Charlie had to be told he was her father, and Riki had to realize he wasn't just having a lusty affair. Someday soon the entire situation would come to a head. He only hoped he'd be able to handle it.

One day he returned home with Charlie and Billy-Jo after taking them on a shopping trip. Each was clutching a brand new doll. He had promised all of the kids something special. He decided to break it into three separate trips after Riki fell off the couch laughing when he told her he was taking all the kids at once.

The downstairs was empty, which was quite unusual for a home with seven children. As he stepped onto the back porch, he spotted all the boys practicing ball. Charlie, Billy-Jo, and Tiny followed him as he headed toward them. One of the twins spotted him, waved, and started running toward him.

"Hi, Travis."

"I'm Trevor."

"Whoever. Where's your mom?"

"In the basement."

"What is she doing there?"

"Don't know. She was in the attic looking for something. The next thing I knew she was running down the steps screaming 'I'll be in the basement.' The slamming of the door was the last thing I heard."

Trevor started to chuckle, then stopped all of a sudden. "Hey, Jason, she was white and all. You don't suppose she saw a ghost up there?"

"No, there are no such things as ghosts."

"You're sure?"

"Positive. Your mother has a problem with attics, that's all." Jason couldn't help it, he started to laugh.

"The last time I seen her turn that color was when me and Travis brought home a garter snake and hid it in the cookie jar."

"You didn't."

"Sure we did."

"What did she do?"

"There was this racket in the kitchen that

sounded like elephants were into the pots. Me and Travis peeked in the door 'cause we figured she was going to kill us. Anyway, she was standing on the kitchen counter throwing pans at it. That poor snake didn't know what to do. It was going around in circles in the middle of the floor. Travis picked it up and took it over to the creek."

Jason had tears running down his face from laughing so hard. He could picture Riki on the counter throwing pans.

"Do us a favor, Jason?"

"Sure."

"Never ask Mom why some of her pots are dented."

He started to laugh again. "Why?"

"Because every time someone does, she sends us to our room."

"Okay." After calming down some, he asked Trevor if he and his brothers would keep an eye on Billy-Jo for a while.

Jason cautiously opened the basement door. If he had learned one thing about Riki, it was that she was unpredictable. The only light came from the single bulb dangling from a rafter. After descending the stairs he spotted her rearranging some canned goods. She was singing a very off-key "Waltzing Matilda." "Riki?"

She jumped two feet straight up. "Jason. Lord, you scared me."

"Sorry, I didn't mean to."

"That's okay."

"You okay?" he asked, concerned. She still looked pale.

"Of course. Just doing a little spring cleaning."

"Why 'Waltzing Matilda'?"

"It's the only song I know from 'Down Under.'"

He opened his arms and she flew into them. "Riki, I know you've been up in the attic." She snuggled tighter against him. "Want to talk about it?"

"What?"

"Why you are frightened of heights." He ran his hand up and down her back, trying to soothe her. At her continued silence, he asked another question. "How long have you been afraid of heights?"

"Since I was five." Her voice was muffled against his chest.

"What happened to you at five?"

"I got stuck in an elevator."

He could barely make out the word elevator. Wouldn't that cause claustrophobia? "How long were you stuck?"

"About half an hour."

"Who was with you, honey?"

"No one. I was alone."

He could feel her shake, and tightened his grip. "It's okay, darling. I've got you. Nothing will hurt you now." He still couldn't connect an elevator with her fear of heights. Then an idea struck. "What floor were you on?"

She let out the most pitiful wail he had ever heard. "The ground floor."

He could feel the front of his shirt becoming damp. She was crying. He continued rubbing her back. He kissed the top of her head and mumbled encouraging words. He still couldn't figure what had prompted the fear. When she stopped crying, he handed her his handkerchief. After she blew her nose and wiped her eyes, he asked, "Better now?" His voice was laced with tenderness and concern.

"Yes, thank you." Her eyes were still pools of sparkling emeralds.

Jason had difficulty clearing his throat. "What was so important in the attic?"

"A surprise."

"For whom?"

"You, silly." She grinned.

"Can I see it?" He was relieved to have his old Riki back.

"Nope, it has to be washed first." She was still grinning.

"When can I see it?" His interest was starting to increase.

"Tonight, if you're a good boy." She leaned over and ran her tongue down the side of his neck.

He grabbed her and kissed her thoroughly. "And if I promise to be a good boy?" His voice was starting to get the husky sound Riki loved.

"If you are real good, your surprise will never be taken off."

She sounded disappointed, and his eyes lit up as the meaning became clear. She ran up the steps and he bellowed after her, "Come back here, wench."

As Jason climbed the maple tree at a quarter to ten, he was still trying to figure out what Riki was up to. All during dinner she had given him knowing looks. That look was designed to turn a sane man crazy, and since he considered himself on the down side of insanity since coming to Virginia, he wondered where that left him.

As he silently stepped over the windowsill, he saw the room was empty. The door was locked, so he figured she must be in the bathroom. Walking over to the closed door, he heard her humming. He couldn't place the tune, but he'd recognize that perfume anywhere. It was Riki. It smelled of jasmine and summer rain.

When he pushed open the bathroom door, he felt like someone hit him in the stomach with a sledgehammer. Riki was standing in the middle of the room, brushing her hair and wearing a corset. It was yellowed with age, but otherwise in perfect condition. There had to be at least fifty tiny pearl buttons down the front, he thought with dismay. Her breasts were pushed up so high, he had no idea why they weren't overflowing the garment. His gaze was glued to that spot for the longest time, then slid to an impossibly thin waist, down past the rounded hips and onto the slender legs. She actually had a garter belt on, with the sheerest white stockings attached. It wasn't the stockings that held his attention. It was the creamy, satin-smooth skin of her upper thighs. His gaze moved past the curving calves to her dainty feet. She wore high heeled slippers with white feathers all over them.

His smoldering gaze started to work its way up. He got as far as her knees when she turned her back to him to give him a better view. He could feel his blood starting to boil. The fire was moving downward, and his jeans were becoming uncomfortable. He took one look at Riki's delectable buttocks and growled.

She glanced over her shoulder and winked. Taking his hand, she led him from the bathroom.

After gently pushing him onto the bed, she knelt down and slipped his sneakers off.

Jason was having a difficult time breathing as he watched her breasts defy gravity. She slowly rose to her feet and turned to the nightstand. Chilled champagne and two crystal glasses stood on top of it. After pouring the champagne and handing Jason a glass, she raised her own.

"Here's to the first six dozen prominent members of the birth control society. May their memory live on into infinity."

Riki never got to taste the champagne. Jason had her pinned to the bed and was kissing her like a dying man. His trembling fingers were trying, without too much success, to unbutton fifty pearl buttons. At one point Riki was trying to help, but he pushed her hands away.

"Didn't they believe in zippers?" he muttered.

"Anticipation."

"Hell, woman, I've been anticipating since the basement."

"Touchy, aren't we?"

"I'll give you touchy."

"Please."

Jason was trying to find his other sneaker as the first ray of dawn slipped into the room. Riki mumbled his name, then rolled over. He was still chuckling when he stepped on a pearl button. Damn, that hurt. As he placed the button with all the others, he wondered how long it would take Riki to sew them back on. He gently kissed her cheek and whispered he loved her. She smiled in her sleep and he slipped out the window.

. . .

"Get your toe out of there." Riki blew at the bubbles floating dangerously close to her nose.

"It got cold," Jason pouted.

"You're going to smell real cute after this."

"Well, you looked so lonesome in here all by yourself. Nothing but a washcloth and a tub full of bubbles for company." He gave her his most innocent smile.

"Jason, please remove your toe immediately. That part of the female anatomy was not designed for toes."

He lunged at her. As he placed wet kisses along her neck, he whispered in his best pirate voice, "Lassie, surely you wound this pirate's heart, thinking he not knoweth where to place his sword."

Riki was giggling and trying to get out of Jason's hold when there was a knock on the bathroom door. "Mom?"

Her eyes opened wide and she smacked her hand over Jason's mouth, not noticing it was covered with bubbles.

"Mommy?"

"Yes, Andrew?"

"I'm thirsty."

"I'm coming."

Jason was spitting out bubbles and glaring at the door. Riki was trying to dry off and put on her robe at the same time. "Didn't you lock the bedroom door?" she whispered fiercely.

"Sorry, I forgot. I seem to have gotten carried away with a vision of a mermaid and her bubbles."

Riki finally got her robe belted and kicked Jason's clothes behind the door. "Duck," she whispered to him.

"Duck?"

"Yes."

"It's full of bubbles."

"Hold your nose."

As Jason went under Riki slipped from the room to take care of Andrew's problem.

"What took you so long, Mom?"

"I was in the tub."

As they headed out of the room, there was a loud splash from the bathroom. Andrew glanced over his shoulder. "What was that?"

"The washcloth must have slipped."

"Must be a big washcloth."

When Riki returned and firmly locked the door behind her, she found Jason in the shower trying to get the bubbles out of his hair. She slipped off her robe and slid open the shower door. "Did I ever tell you about this fantasy I have about a pirate, his sword, and a waterfall?"

Riki's back was toward the door as she was making peanut butter and jelly sandwiches for the kids' lunches. Jason silently crossed the floor. He wrapped his arms around her waist and nuzzled her neck. Feeling her relax and bend her neck forward to give him better access increased his desire.

"Perfect morning, darlin'," he whispered in her ear before taking a nip at the lobe. "I hate to tell you this, but there's a strange man in your garage."

"Mmm, that's nice."

Jason couldn't suppress a chuckle. What was

he going to do with her? He knew what he would like to do with her, but with seven kids running around screaming, fighting, and downing Fruit Loops like the bottom was going to drop out of the sugar market, he'd have to show some semblance of control.

"I mean it, Riki. There's a strange old man in there fiddling with your riding mower." When all he received was a seductive smile, he roared, "Dammit, Riki, say something." His voice lowered in disgust, "He called me 'Sonny.' "

As royally as any queen brandishing her scepter, she waved a knife dripping grape jelly. "Off with his head." A momentary lull in the children's uproar and a quiet chuckle from Jason were the only rewards she received for her acting. She muttered under her breath about everybody being a critic nowadays.

"I gather," Jason said, "that this little piece of information doesn't bother you?"

She kissed the corner of his mouth. "Of course it does, Jason. The nerve of his calling you 'Sonny.' As soon as I'm done here I'll go have a talk with that man."

"Riki, do you know who that man is?"

"Yes, Jason. That's Harold. He and his wife, Norma, live across the street."

"What's he doing in your garage messing with your mower?"

"We have an agreement. If he mows my yard with my mower, he's allowed to use it for his yard."

"Why?"

"Jason, Harold is not a young man anymore. He

had a stroke two years ago, and he really shouldn't be pushing a mower in this heat."

"So what's that got to do with your mower? Why doesn't he go out and buy a riding mower?"

Using the tone of voice she reserved for lecturing naughty children, she asked, "Jason, darling, do Harold and Norma look like they could afford to go right out and buy a riding mower?"

As Jason pictured the weather-beaten, sagging-porch house across the street he had to agree with Riki. "No."

"Well, then, why not let him use my mower? Besides, who else is going to drive it?" At Jason's raised brows, she resumed packing lunches and mumbled, "I don't know how."

Chuckling under his breath, he pictured Riki buying a riding mower just so her neighbor didn't have to push his. Come to think of it, it wasn't such a bad arrangement after all. Just to be on the safe side he'd go have a talk with sweet old Harold and check out the mower.

After a conversation with Harold, who did turn out to be a sweet old man, Jason started forming an idea in the dark recesses of his mind. The more he thought about it, the better he liked it. He twisted it, turned it upside down and inside out, but he could find no major flaw with it. It was the obvious solution to the dilemma he and Riki found themselves in.

Joy shot through him at the thought of telling her about his plan. But on second thought, he'd proceed with the idea and tell her about it when it was set in concrete. Then she couldn't dispute his love. She'd have to marry him. He had a lot of phone calls to make, appointments to keep, and a brick walk to finish.

Most importantly he had to keep Riki busy enough that she wouldn't notice he was up to something. The future looked fantastic. With renewed confidence and a determined step, he marched off to the study to put his plan into action.

Two days later the inevitable happened. Sam called. He needed Jason home immediately or an important deal would go under. Riki found Jason in her study raking his hand through his hair and with papers spread out all over her desk. He watched the light fade from her eyes while he told her he had to take the morning flight to Dallas. It was like ripping out his own heart. Promising it would only take two or three days didn't seem to brighten the situation. Grabbing her by the shoulders and kissing the socks off her did bring a smile to her lips, but somehow that smile never made it to her eyes.

Telling the kids before they went to bed was bad enough, but when Charlie disappeared from the room, he practically went nuts. They found her curled up in the fetal position on her bed, staring at a blank wall.

Riki remained in the doorway, motioning for Jason to go to Charlie. When he sat on the edge of the bed and started to explain that it was only for two days, maybe three, he didn't get any response. Charlie's silver eyes didn't so much as blink. When he gently touched her shoulder, she cringed. Turning tear-filled eyes toward Riki, he silently asked her for help.

She crossed to the other side of the bed and sat

down. When she tenderly brushed back a tendril of Charlie's hair from her face, she was unprepared for the child's reaction. She hurled herself at Riki. Small skinny arms circled her waist as a pale urchin face pressed into her breasts. Riki's arms instinctively wrapped Charlie in a protective embrace. Softly rocking back and forth and whispering soothing words, she dared to glance at Jason.

The color had drained from his face. As he rose to leave with Charlie still clinging to her, she noticed the total dejection in his eyes. Reaching out a hand to him, she wasn't surprised when he whispered a harsh "No." He walked out of the room with his head bowed and shoulders slumped, not seeing the tears streaming down her face.

She continued rocking and whispering to Charlie until she felt the girl's arms loosen their hold and her breath settle into an even rhythm. Turning down the covers she lay Charlie in the center of the bed and tucked her in. After stopping in her bathroom to wash her tearstained face and try to compose herself, she went downstairs to round up the rest of the troops. It was past their bedtime.

While tucking in all the Munchkins, she promised them she would wake them up early so they could say good-bye to Jason before he left.

She found Jason in the study, systematically emptying the bottle of Scotch. He was pouring a mouthful into a glass, downing it in one gulp, then repeating the process.

"Trying to get drunk?"

"Yes."

"Why?"

"You saw what happened. My own daughter can't stand for me to touch her."

She crossed the room to pour herself an apricot brandy. "Is that how you saw it?"

"That's how it was!" His voice was low and harsh. "Don't start to analyze me, Riki. I know what I saw."

"Yes, but do you understand what you saw?"

She didn't quite catch what he muttered under his breath. Watching him down the third drink since she walked into the room, she decided it was time to explain before he became too intoxicated to understand. "Listen, Jason, I don't tell you how to build a building and you don't tell me how to understand children. I won't analyze you because adults aren't my cup of tea. Personally, I think all adults have a few screws loose. That's what life does to us all. It's children who fascinate me. They haven't learned yet to throw up decoy barriers. Their emotions are basically straightforward, except for the few like Charlie. She's lost the ability to express her feelings." Making sure she still had Jason's attention, she asked, "Do you have any idea what your child is feeling?"

"Repulsion."

Knowing Jason was being sarcastic to cover up his hurt calmed her own nerves. She took a small sip of brandy to fortify herself. "No, Jason. Your daughter is scared."

"Of me?"

"Yes."

"What does she think I'm going to do, beat her?" His hand was trembling as he reached for his glass, and she knew she had to do something before he became totally drunk.

"No," she said. "Put down that drink and I'll tell you what Charlie is afraid of." His eyes darted between her and the glass, but he did replace the glass on the desk. "Thank you. Charlie is scared you are going to leave and not return. More than likely she connects it to her mother and stepfather leaving and never returning again."

As Jason ran his fingers through his hair he seemed to come to some kind of decision. "That's settled then. I'm not going to Dallas in the morning. The deal can just fall through. Charlie is more important to me than a major deal any day."

"I'm glad you said that. But I think you will be making a major mistake. She has got to learn that the people she loves, and for some unknown reason she has taken a fancy to you, will come back."

"But does it have to be now?"

"What better time? She's here with us, she knows we all love her. She's comfortable here. I'm here. Can you honestly say that once she's in Dallas with you, you'll never have to leave her? Who would you leave her with, your sister? Charlie doesn't even know her. Now is as good a time as any, Jason."

He thought about all the plans he had been making. Was now the time to tell Riki? He thought about future business trips to Dallas and realized the problem would still exist even if all his plans went through. "Okay, I'll go."

"Thank you."

"For what?"

"Trusting me with your daughter."

He rose from his chair and crossed the room to stand directly in front of her. Lifting her chin so that she could read the truth in his eyes, he said, "I love you, Erika. I trust you with my life."

Her reply was lost in the crush of lips. Heat spread through her body, matched by the growing arousal of the man she loved. Hearing her moan, he broke the kiss. Running his lips down the side of her neck, he muttered, "Please don't make me climb that damn tree tonight, not tonight, darlin'."

"No, Jason, not tonight. Not ever again," was her heated declaration.

The next morning, half an hour before the kids were normally up, they all stood on the front porch dressed in their pajamas, except for Riki who wore blue jeans and a Garfield T-shirt for such a festive occasion. Personally, she'd seen more excitement at a wake. If this was how they acted when Jason left for only two or three days, she thought, she couldn't imagine what it would do to them when he went for good.

And if their desperate lovemaking last night and early this morning was anything to go by, she had no idea what she would do. As he said goodbye to the boys, he made them promise to take care of their mom until he got back. He promised them each something special if they all behaved and listened to her.

Picking up a sleepy-eyed Billy-Jo, he received a sloppy kiss on the side of his neck. He set her on her feet, then patted Tiny on the head, ordering him to watch over his big girl Charlie until he returned.

Kneeling down in front of Charlie, he felt a lump suddenly catch in his throat. She was hiding behind Riki, her arms wrapped around Riki's legs, her face buried in the folds of the Garfield T-shirt. Placing his hand on her slim shoulder, he whispered bye-bye and told her to take care of herself. If she did her homework she would get a surprise when he returned. Receiving no response, he slowly straightened to face the hardest good-bye. Riki.

Seeing the tears in her eyes almost caused him to cancel the whole trip. She accurately read the look on his face and whispered, "Go, please."

His mouth touched hers in a kiss that promised the future, and held a hint of desperation. "I can't say good-bye to you, darlin'," he said, the words torn from his throat. "So, I leave you with I love you." After a last quick kiss, he turned and walked briskly to his car.

He had his hand on the door handle when a rusty, hoarse, squeaky voice split the air. "Daddy, don't go." He spun around to see his daughter standing on the edge of the porch with her arms stretched out to him. As he dropped his bag and ran back up the brick walk, he vaguely noticed the openmouthed stares his daughter was getting.

When he reached the bottom step, Charlie hurled herself from the porch straight into his open arms. With tears of happiness streaming down his face, he twirled his daughter around in circles. She had talked.

With Charlie's arms and legs wrapped around him in a fierce grip, he studied the other children. They were just recovering their vocal cords.

"Hey, Charlie talked."

"Why did she call Jason Daddy?"

"Always knew she could talk."

"Would someone please tell me what's happening?"

"Sorry, Jake. Jason's holding Charlie now."

"Why?"

"I guess because she spoke."

It was Tiny's bark that drew Jason's attention back to Riki. "She spoke." With a look of pride, love, and great accomplishment on his face he said, "She called me. Did you hear that?"

Blinking back tears that threatened to spill at any moment, Riki said, "Yes, I heard, but did you hear what she called you?" At Jason's blank look she answered her own question. "Daddy."

"Well, of course. I am her father."

"How did she know that?"

Looking down at the small dark head pressed against his chest, he started to wonder the same thing. "I don't know."

"Hey, wow, did you hear that? Jason's Charlie's father."

"Neat-oh."

"I wish he was my dad."

Riki looked at her youngest son and wondered how much he missed having a father. He was too young to remember Brad. Hearing the chorus of agreements didn't help to lighten her heavy heart. Jason was going back to Dallas. Charlie knew he was her father. There was nothing to hold him in Virginia any longer. Well, just great, she told herself. Why don't you get mad at the poor little girl for finally talking?

She shooed the children into the house, ordering them to dress for school. She told Billy-Jo to go find a doll and feed her breakfast, knowing that it would keep her busy for a while. Then she led Jason, who still had Charlie clutched in his arms, into the front parlor and sat on the sofa. He sat beside her and lifted Charlie's chin. For the first time in seven months, Riki noticed tears gathering in the usually vague silver eyes.

Jason had to swallow the lump in his throat before he could speak. "Hi," he said huskily.

He received a hesitant smile and a rusty "Hi" back. Folding Charlie in his arms and giving her a huge hug, he thanked the Lord for his daughter.

Riki moved closer to the clinging pair. "Charlie, honey?" The child lifted her face. "How did you know Jason is your daddy?"

Small frightened eyes darted between Riki and Jason before she buried her face in Jason's shirt front. As he gathered her closer, he shot Riki a look that clearly said, "Knock it off." Never one to back away when there were unanswered questions, she plowed on.

"It's okay, Charlie. You're allowed to know that Jason's your father. In fact, I'm very happy you know and I'm sure Jason is too. Do you see the way he's holding you? He's not mad. He's very proud to be your daddy."

Charlie raised her head to look at a smiling Jason, then turned to Riki.

"All we want to know," Riki said, "is how you know that Jason is your daddy." As Charlie stared blankly at her, she changed tactics. "Did your mommy tell you?" Charlie shook her head no. "Did your daddy Richard tell you?" Again the small head shook. "Did you know that Jason was your daddy when he first came here?" This time she nodded.

Riki glanced at Jason and he shrugged. "That explains the immediate acceptance," she said.

"Thanks a lot," he muttered. Receiving a sweet smile and a 'You're welcome' in return didn't seem to pacify him.

Riki returned her attention to Charlie. "Honey, do you think you could tell us how you knew?"

The look on Charlie's face was one of total concentration as she searched her mind for the right word. "Book."

Jason's and Riki's response coincided with each other. "Book?"

Charlie slid from Jason's lap and searched the room until she found what she was looking for, a magazine. She placed it on Riki's lap. Riki glanced at the books lining her shelves, a pile of children's books on the coffee table, and the family photo albums stacked haphazardly on the lowest shelf. Obviously Charlie knew what she was searching for, a magazine. But why?

Jason's face cleared as a sudden thought occurred to him. "Charlie, did you see my picture in a magazine? Was I standing in front of a big truck?" Charlie nodded. "Did your mommy and daddy Richard see the picture too?" Damn, he thought. That man's name left a rotten taste in his mouth. Again the child nodded. "What happened when they saw it?"

Charlie looked down and bit her lower lip. Finally she raised tear-filled eyes and whispered, "Yelled."

Jason closed his eyes as pain twisted in his heart. Why did his sweet innocent daughter have to suffer because of thoughtless adults?

He took a deep breath and asked, "Do you remember any words that they yelled?" He was almost afraid to contemplate what kind of words could have been shouted. His heart stopped when his daughter answered, "Money."

Riki watched as Jason closed his eyes and hugged his daughter tighter. She heard him whisper how sorry he was and that nothing was ever going to hurt her again. What kind of woman was this Cynthia? she wondered. What kind of man was Richard? How could they have kept Charlie from her father? Were they going to demand money from him? Considering the neighborhood Charlie had been living in, it was a definite possibility.

As she saw two tears slide down Jason's cheek, anger burned in the pit of her stomach. How could they have done this to Jason? They'd had no right to keep Charlie from him. Maybe they had changed their minds and were not going to demand money. "Charlie honey, when did they see the picture?"

Charlie lifted her face from Jason's neck. Riki noticed the tears and quivering lip, and her heart bled. "Day they went away."

As the words registered, Riki stared at Jason. The color drained from his face as a look of helplessness overtook his features. He'd never know if they were going to call and demand money. He could have known about Charlie months ago, if they hadn't been killed in the accident. All those wasted months, all those wasted years!

Riki placed a box of tissues beside Jason and told him she'd see to breakfast. All the kids were eating and she was making French toast when Jason and Charlie walked into the room. Both were smiling.

"I'm not going to Dallas," Jason said.

"Why?"

"I can't leave Charlie now." By his tone of voice it was clear he thought she was a few bricks shy of a full load.

"How much money are you going to lose?"

He shuffled his feet and seemed fascinated by the pattern on the linoleum. "Profit?" he muttered.

"Is there anything else?"

When he named a figure that stopped Riki's heart, she wanted to cry. Not that he was losing all that money, but his little construction company just took on gigantic proportions. How could he ever give that up and start again in Virginia? Here she was visualizing him sitting at her desk figuring out additions, new roofs, and the cost of adding an extra bathroom. What would he ever do in Mountain View? With what he was losing on this one deal, he could put a down payment on the entire town.

Jason saw the tears gather in Riki's eyes and quickly crossed the floor to pull her into his arms. "It's okay, Riki, I won't go broke." Hearing a muffled response against his chest, he added, "I'll think of something if it's so important to you, darlin'." As he rocked Riki in his arms, his gaze never strayed from Charlie who was busy eating Cheerios.

An idea slowly formed in his mind. It would work, but Riki would never agree to it. A slow smile curved his mouth as he spotted seven partners in crime. It really wasn't fair to Riki, but all was fair in love and war.

He cleared his throat and practically shouted, "Hey, everyone!" When he had the attention of the kids, he asked, "How would you all like to go to Dallas for a few days?" When he received blank stares and open mouths, he clarified, "You know, in a big airplane. You can all sleep at my place."

In the next instant he wished for those opened-mouthed stares. How could seven children cause such a racket? Between the exuberant shouts and questions he could feel Riki drawing back. When he saw the stubborn tilt of her chin and the determination in her lovely eyes, he knew he had a battle on his hands. She opened her mouth and quite firmly said, "No."

This brought immediate quiet to the room. "Why?" he asked.

She stated the most obvious answer. "School."

Jason looked at the kids. "Is anyone doing so badly at school that he can't afford to miss three days of it?" When Riki answered "no," he pinned the boys and Charlie with a stern look. "Is everyone in agreement that when we get back from Dallas you will make up all classwork and homework with no complaints?" Receiving five nods, he turned back to Riki and raised an eyebrow.

"Tiny and Dust Ball," she said.

"Don't you have a neighbor who would look after them?"

"Harold looked after them when we went camping," Travis shouted.

"Next objection," Jason said.

Riki racked her brain for any possible objections. The best she could come up with was, "Money. Do you have any idea what it would cost to fly us all down to Dallas for three days?"

"That's peanuts compared to what I lose if I don't go. And I won't leave Charlie here. Do you think she could handle being at my sister's day and night for three days while I'm in meetings?"

"No."

"Neither do I, Riki. I want you and all the kids to come to Dallas with me. I would like you to meet my sister, Stella, and her family. You'll like them. I want them to get to know Charlie and all of you." He ran his index finger over her lower lip. "Please, for me."

How could a woman refuse that? she asked herself. Glancing at the clock she saw the children had already missed their buses. If she went to Dallas it would mean three more days with Jason. She cupped his cheek and answered, "For you, anything."

A shiver slid down his spine and he crushed Riki to his chest. "Thank you, darlin'."

To say that Jason was a "mover and a shaker" was probably the understatement of the century. Within four hours Riki found herself and seven smiling children on a 727 bound for Dallas.

Ten

Three days later Jason awakened in the same state of mind as when he had gone to bed—frustrated. The past few days had been pure hell. Sleeping an average of four hours per night in a cold lonely bed while Riki was in the next room wasn't his idea of fun. He rarely saw Charlie, only for a couple of minutes before he had to leave to attend an unrelenting parade of business meetings.

After a quick cool shower to try to take the bite out of his frustration, he entered the kitchen. So much for privacy, he thought. All seven children were present and discussing the upcoming trip to the aquarium.

Riki had her back toward the door as she fried bacon. At the sound of Charlie shouting "Daddy," she turned around. Jason was standing in the doorway looking at her with desire burning in his eyes. Pure joy shot through her. Her gaze dropped to his mouth. Lord, how she wanted that mouth.

Jason watched a smile form on her lips, watched

her eyes start to shine with happiness. He stood very still as her gaze traveled from his face and down past the silk tie that was suddenly choking him. Then he saw the happiness in her eyes replaced with sadness and a touch of pain. He stood there helplessly as the smile died.

This was the Jason who lived in Dallas, Riki thought. This was the Jason who owned a condo that probably cost three times as much as her whole house. He wasn't the same Jason who fixed her brick walk, who helped coach the boys' T-ball team, and who made incredible love to her all through the night.

The man standing in front of her was a successful businessman from the top of his still-damp black hair to the tips of his handmade leather shoes. This man was a shaker and a mover. He owned a business so large, she was still having problems handling it. There was no other way to explain it. Jason was downright rich.

Add being rich to his list of sins, she thought. That included being handsome and charming, possessing a great sense of humor, and being the cream of the crop as far as lovers go, and it all added up to zero.

She looked down. Seeing her new white sneakers, she grimaced. Boy, she must really look lovely, dressed in jeans and a sleeveless yellow top. When you go sightseeing with seven children, you have to dress for comfort and the hell with fashion. Now, standing in front of Jason, who was dressed in a suit that definitely did not come off the rack, she fought the incredible urge to excuse herself and change into something formal.

Jason instinctively moved forward to embrace

and comfort Riki. He had taken two steps when his daughter stepped in front of him. He kneeled down and opened his arms to gather up his child. When she hesitated, he softly called her name.

With both hands behind her back, she stared down at the floor. "I bought you something." Her voice was so low, he had trouble hearing her.

He looked up at Riki. She smiled, and he returned his attention to Charlie. "You did?"

"You read us a story about a lion who had a thorn stuck in his foot." He nodded. "You said that when you were little like me, you always wanted a lion."

"So I did."

Charlie brought her hands out from behind her back. Nestled in them was a stuffed lion, who looked more comical than fierce. His heart overflowing with love, he took the lion from her. This was his first gift from his daughter. How many Father's Days had he missed? What about birthday cards done by hand with crayons? The mangy mane of the lion blurred as his eyes filled with tears. He tried desperately to swallow the lump in his throat. Somehow this cross-eyed lion with the lopsided grin took away all the bitterness he was feeling for being deprived of his daughter for six years.

Gathering Charlie into his arms, he buried his face in her hair until he gained some semblance of control. He stood back up and swung her around in a circle. As she smiled he said, "I love you, Charleen Nesbit."

Her small arms encircled his neck and her lips brushed across his cheek. Then he heard her whisper, "I love you too, Daddy." Joy exploded within him at those simple words. It seemed he had waited a lifetime for them.

His whole world brightened. The only dark spot was Riki. What was bothering her? Whatever it was, he'd take care of it as soon as they were back home. He knew she loved him. There was just no way she could be so responsive to his every touch if she didn't. But this was not the right time or place to talk with her about their future. She had been nervous and upset since coming to Dallas. In fact, if he didn't know better, he'd swear she was avoiding him. Since he had definite plans to spend the entire night tonight in her brass bed nestled in the foothills of the Blue Ridge Mountains, it would be kind of hard for her to pretend he wasn't there.

He returned his thoughts to his daughter, who was still clinging to his neck. "Thank you, sweetheart. He's the most handsome lion I have ever seen. Does he have a name?" She shook her head. "Would you like to help me name him?" As her little head bobbed up and down, he felt that motion was connected to his heart.

He watched in amusement as her small brow furrowed in concentration. When she made no suggestions he supplied one. "How about Leo?" Her little nose wrinkled up in apparent contempt, and he burst out laughing. "Okay, so you don't like Leo. Do you have a better suggestion?"

"Roar."

"Why Roar?"

"Mommy-Riki told me that's what he says."

He glanced questioningly at Riki. "She wanted to know what to call me," Riki said. "Mrs. McCormick made me sound like an old lady. Do you mind?"

"No. In fact, I kind of like it, Mommy-Riki." He smiled at her, then at Charlie. "And I like 'Roar.' " He held the cross-eyed lion up and announced that Roar was going to the office today with him. This statement brought forth a fit of giggles from his daughter and from the six children watching from the dining room table.

"What's the matter?" he asked. "Do you think Roar will scare my secretary?" Receiving more laughter, he held the lion up to his nose. He crossed his eyes and proceeded to lecture Roar on office etiquette. When all the laughter died down, he saw he was running late. He'd sacrifice breakfast any day to hear his daughter laugh like this morning. Now if only he could make Riki laugh again.

He affectionately ruffled the boys' hair, quickly kissed the girls, and warned them all to behave themselves for their mother. As he passed Riki he latched on to her wrist and pulled her into the living room with him. He positioned her with her back against the door. His trembling hand cupped her chin and forced her to look at him. "I've missed you."

No sweeter words ever touched Riki's ears. She clasped the back of his head, her gaze as heated as his. "I've missed you too," she whispered while she applied downward pressure to his head.

Jason didn't need much urging. He met Riki's waiting lips with a kiss that held three days of pent-up frustration. He felt her soft and yielding body pressed against his and almost lost control.

What was he thinking of? There were seven

children in the next room and he was going to be late for his meeting. Whenever he kissed Riki, he lost all sense of time and place. At least the kiss answered one question. Riki still wanted him.

He stepped away from her and bent down to retrieve Roar, who had landed on the floor during the embrace. He slowly straightened, giving himself time to regain some control over his emotions. He knew Riki was experiencing the same desire that surged through his body. They would work out whatever was bothering her when they got back home, he vowed silently. They had to. "Darlin', I don't know what's been bothering you, but we will straighten it out tonight back home, okay?"

She nodded. He kissed the end of her nose and left. Somehow it just seemed right that he walked out the door carrying a crazy lion.

Jason downed the remaining Scotch in his glass while staring unseeingly out into the Virginia night. It had been a mistake to take Riki and the kids to Dallas, he thought. Charlie was on her way to becoming a little chatterbox. The boys and Billy-Jo had had a real blast visiting museums and sightseeing. Riki had been the mistake. She had grown more withdrawn every day.

Since they had arrived back in Virginia earlier that evening, she hadn't said more than a dozen words to him. After tucking all the kids into their beds for the night, he asked to see her for a moment in her study. She explained she had a couple of things to handle first, but she'd be right down.

He knew the moment she walked into the room. An inner alarm went off in his body. His heart beat picked up, his arms ached to hold her, and his jeans became uncomfortable with embarrassing speed. Maybe throwing this surprise on her wasn't such a good idea after all. He should have let her in on it from the beginning. It was her future too. What was going to happen if she totally disagreed with all the plans? He'd have to play his trump card, Charlie. There was no way Riki would throw a homeless child out into the street.

As of this afternoon Charlie had no permanent home. Jason had signed the agreement of sale on his condo in Dallas. Charlie also had an unemployed father. Granted, her father still owned a substantial share of stock in a construction company in Dallas, but all major decisions were to be handled by her uncle Sam.

As the silence stretched between them and the tension took on a life force of its own, Jason became more and more convinced he had made an error in judgment. He slowly turned from the darkness of the night to gaze at his sunshine, Riki. She looked incredibly nervous. He silently weighed his options and decided the direct approach was the best.

He set his empty glass down on the desk, cleared his throat, opened his arms, and asked, "Riki, will you marry me?"

His arms slowly lowered to his side as pain filled Riki's eyes.

Her heart shouted *Yes!* Her mind roared *No!* Not now, not enough time. Never enough time. She would love Jason with her last breath, would go to her grave loving him, but she couldn't marry him. It had taken months of love and understanding to get her sons to accept the fact that their father was never coming home again and that this was their new home. She had vowed two years ago never to uproot her family again. Some promises were meant to be broken, and for the love she felt for Jason she'd break that vow in a moment.

The promise she had made Jake and Pete couldn't be broken, though. How could she possibly adopt them legally from the state of Virginia if she were married and living in Texas? She had had to get permission from the state even to take them to Dallas for three days. What would they say if she told them she was moving there?

She couldn't take a chance the state would make an exception to the rule for her. She'd been caught up in bureaucratic red tape before. Sometimes the tape was so thick it smothered little people like Jake and Pete.

With tears in her eyes, she whispered the words that would condemn Jason to a life of loneliness and despair. "I'm sorry, I can't."

"Why? You love me."

"Yes, I love you." She crossed her arms and hugged herself as tears slipped down her cheeks. "Please, Jason, don't make this harder on me."

He watched those tears in total bewilderment. Yes, she loved him, no, she wouldn't marry him. Nothing was making any sense. "Okay, Riki, I'll let the subject drop for tonight if you tell me why."

She tried to gain control and took a deep breath. "Promises."

"To whom?"

"Jake and Pete."

"What promises did you make to Jake and Pete?"

"That I'm adopting them. I'll become their real mother." When Jason stared at her as if she was a candidate for the funny farm, she explained further. "How in the hell do you expect me to adopt them in the state of Virginia when we'll be living in Texas? It's on file that I'm a single parent with four children living in rural Virginia. What do you think will happen when I turn up married with five children and living in a two-bedroom condominium in Dallas, Texas? Do you have any idea what kind of investigation they have done on me? Dammit, they don't let just anyone adopt kids."

Joy flooded through Jason's body as her words started to make sense. Riki was afraid of losing Pete and Jake when they moved to Texas. Well, since he wasn't planning on moving Riki and the children to Texas, that eliminated her reason for saying no.

"Why, Erika, I believe that's the first time I ever heard you cuss." Grinning broadly, he added, "I really don't think it's appropriate for a mother of seven to use such language."

As he leaned casually back against the wall, Riki searched her mind for the reason behind his silly grin. She'd just turned down his proposal and he was grinning. For that matter, why had he called her a mother of seven? When he left with Charlie, that would leave her with six. He was definitely up to something. "Do you know something I don't?"

The grin faded from his face. "I'm afraid there's quite a bit you don't know. When I was in Texas I signed papers selling my condo. I also sold a major portion of my construction company to my brother-in-law, Sam. I still own the majority of the stock in the company, but Sam's going to run it."

"But what are you going to do?"

"I've had a couple of preliminary meetings with Dave Moyer at the Mountain View High School. Come September I'll be starting a new construction company geared to hire teenagers who are willing to work half a day and go to school in the mornings. Since the kids will all be trainees, we can afford to offer our services at a very reasonable rate. Many of the senior citizens will be able to afford us."

He watched as a smile started at the corners of Riki's mouth. "Of course, I won't be making megabucks, but with a little conservation I might be able to support a wife and seven children."

Her smile turned into a full-blown grin. "With a real frugal wife you might be able to support eight kids."

His gaze slid down to her waist and he visualized Riki carrying his child under her heart. "Definitely eight."

Riki's eyes turned passionate as she imagined all the ways they could go about making number eight. "Ask me again."

Without a moment of hesitation Jason asked Riki to become his wife for the second time within ten minutes. The question was barely out of his mouth when she shouted "Yes" and flew across the room into his waiting arms.

He hugged her fiercely. "When?"

With tears of joy and love in her eyes, she answered, "Today, tomorrow. How about yesterday?" She stroked his cheeks and whispered, "I love you, Jason Nesbit."

"I love you, Erika McCormick soon to be Nesbit."

Their lips met in a soft, tender kiss that held the promise of tomorrow. When Riki's arms twined around Jason's neck, the kiss turned hot and hungry. His tongue plunged into her mouth the same instant his hands cupped her bottom and brought her hard against his arousal.

He heard her groan and swung her up into his arms. "Do you think all the kids are asleep?"

"After a day like today, I'm sure they are." She ran her tongue up his jaw and nipped at his ear. She felt him shudder and added, "How would you like to walk up the steps instead of climbing a tree?"

With a chuckle Jason declared he was feeling kind of animalistic. With Riki still cradled in his arms he walked out of the room. He'd just bent his head for another kiss when a sound stopped him in his tracks.

"Oh, yuck!"

"They're kissing again. Told you."

"They're allowed. They said they're getting married."

"Does that make Jason our dad?"

There on the stairs sat all seven children, grinning as they peered through the railing. Riki stared at the children and started to laugh. "I guess the peanut gallery approves. Shall we take a vote? All those in favor of Jason becoming their dad and me becoming Charlie's mom say 'aye.' "

When the noise level threatened to wake the neighbors, Jason whistled loudly to regain some order. With a reluctant sigh he released Riki until she was standing on her own two feet. He bent and whispered in her ear, "Whatever you do, darlin', don't shut that window tonight."

Epilogue

Riki quietly walked past the kitchen, afraid to break the unusual silence of the house. With the six older children is school and Billy-Jo attending her weekly 'Teaching for Tots' class, Jason was sure to be in the study. She couldn't figure out why he worked so hard on his requests. The school board would grant him anything he asked. He had single-handedly stopped three kids from dropping out of school, and it was only October. His home improvement company was flourishing. Senior citizens were lining up to get work done by the Half Day Construction Company.

As the study doors loomed in front of her, she wondered how good Jason's sense of humor was. In the past five months of marriage, she'd noticed his humor always came before any signs of temper. Nothing seemed to rattle him. Well, there always was a first time.

Maybe she was making too big a deal out of it. Jason obviously knew the risk when he stopped using contraceptives on their wedding night. At her questioning glance, he'd declared he was tired of making love with a raincoat on. Now five months later those tiny rain drops had turned into a full-fledged flood. Two floods, to be exact. When her doctor had told her she was carrying Travis and Trevor, no one had been more shocked than she. Twins didn't run in either hers or Brad's families. They thought it was a twist of fate. After the test today to confirm she was once again carrying twins, she guessed the blame was on her shoulders.

Jason glanced up as Riki entered the study. The first thing he noticed was how she avoided his eyes. She was nervously playing with a tendril of hair and doing an excellent imitation of pacing. He crossed his arms behind his head and leaned back in the chair. Maybe she was finally going to tell him. He'd guessed two weeks ago he was going to become a father again, for the eighth time. He just couldn't figure out why she hadn't announced it before now.

He watched her walk from the window to the bookshelves. When she picked up a book and started leafing through it, he decided enough was enough. She was obviously upset and that couldn't be good for their baby. Maybe he should just tell her he knew, then demand to know why she waited so long to tell him. He was just opening his mouth when she asked, "Jason, do you like children?"

He couldn't help it. He burst out laughing. When he got himself under control, he said, "Darlin', in case you've forgotten, we have seven children."

"Let me rephrase that. Do you like babies?"

"Ahhh. Do you mean those tiny little pink things that either seem to cry or sleep? Those little people who always seem to need their diaper changed or to be burped?"

"Yes, them."

"Well, I can't say that I like them." At Riki's look of dismay, he continued, "They don't have any teeth or manners."

Her mouth fell open. When she realized she resembled a big-mouth bass, she snapped it shut. He knew! she thought. And he was baiting her. But she still had one up on him. There was no way he could know it was twins. She and her doctor had just found out an hour ago.

She walked over to him. He pulled her onto his lap and kissed her. She was the first one to break the kiss before it bloomed into something more. She still had one more thing to do.

Reaching out, she ran her finger over his bottom lip. "You knew?" At his nod she asked, "How?"

While he explained all the signs that had given her away, she studied the smile that turned up the corners of his mouth. When he finished she asked, "Are you happy?"

"I've never been happier in my life. Well, maybe on our wedding night, but this is definitely second best. I love babies, especially ours." He cupped her gently rounded tummy. "Good lord, eight kids. That's a nice even number, don't you think?" She mumbled something into his neck. "I have two favors to ask," he continued. "One is I want extra help for the house, at least until the baby is old enough. The second is if it's a girl can we please name her something that sounds like a girl?"

"I'll think about it." She playfully bit his earlobe. "Do you want to see a picture of our baby?"

He chuckled. "Sure. An eight-by-ten glossy would be nice."

"You have to settle for a black-and-white Polaroid."

At his bemused expression, she reached into the back pocket of her jeans and withdrew a small snapshot. She handed it to Jason, who stared at the different shapes of pale gray to dark gray. He glanced from Riki back to the picture in his hand.

"Jason dear, have you ever heard of ultrasound?"

"Yeah, sure."

"This picture was taken an hour ago at General Hospital. Pretty good likeness, don't you think?"

"Why?"

"Well, you are the father. It would be strange if the child didn't even look like me or you."

"Riki, why was this picture taken? Is this a normal practice or is something wrong?" He stopped looking at the picture and devoted his whole attention to his wife. Something wasn't right. He could feel it deep within. She should have told him weeks ago she was pregnant. Was something wrong with the baby? Was Riki in danger?

She correctly read the concern in his eyes. "No, dear, everything and everyone is just fine. We're in perfect A-1 shape." She turned the picture upside down from the way he'd been holding it. "You see this cute little gray blob? That's our baby."

He studied the picture and grinned. "I don't think our child will like being called a blob, cute or otherwise."

"Yes, but that's neither here nor there. Now you see that cute little gray blob?" She pointed to an identical marking not far from the first. "That's our baby too."

His eyes widened and Riki held her breath. He tore his gaze from the picture to her face. When he read the truth there he dropped his gaze to her stomach. *Two! My lord, there are two!*

"Twins?" When all he received in answer was a serene smile, he looked at the picture again. "Are there any more cute little gray blobs?"

"No, Jason, just those two."

"Twins." He raked a hand through his hair. "Shouldn't you be off your feet?"

She giggled. "I am off my feet, in case you haven't noticed." She swung her sneaker-clad feet in the air. His arms instinctively tightened around her.

"Shouldn't you be in bed or something?"

She brushed her mouth against his. "I thought you'd never ask."

When she started to unbutton his shirt he muttered, "Are you sure we can do this?"

"We'd better do it now, because in about five to six months we won't be able to."

She ran her tongue over his lower lip. With a groan of desire, he stood with her in his arms and headed for the stairs.

"Twins," he said once more. "How did we ever do that?"

"That's what happens when you go out into the rain without your raincoat on."

THE EDITOR'S CORNER

Next month we celebrate our sixth year of publishing LOVESWEPT. Behind the scenes, the original team still works on the line with undiminished enthusiasm and pride. Susann is a full editor now, Nita is still the "fastest reader in the East or West," Barbara has written every single piece of back-cover copy (except the three I wrote in the first month, only proving Barbara should do them all), and from afar Elizabeth still edits one or two books each month. And I believe I can safely say that our authors' creative contributions and continuing loyalty to the line is unparalleled. From book #1 (**HEAVEN'S PRICE** by Sandra Brown) to book #329 (next month's **WAITING FOR LILA** by Billie Green) and on into the future, our authors consistently give us their best work and earn our respect and affection more each day.

Now, onward and upward for at least six more great years, here are some wonderful LOVESWEPT birthday presents for you. Joan Elliott Pickart leads off with **TO FIRST BE FRIENDS**, LOVESWEPT #324. Shep Templeton was alive! The award-winning journalist, the only man Emily Templeton had ever loved, hadn't died in the Pataguam jungle, but was coming home—only to learn his wife had divorced him. Eight months before, after a night of reckless passion, he had left for his dangerous assignment. She'd vowed then it was the last time Shep would leave her. Love for Emily was all that had kept Shep going, had made him want to live through months of pain and recovery. Now he had to fight for a new start. . . . Remember, this marvelous book is also available in a beautiful hardcover collector's edition from Doubleday.

In **BOUND TO HAPPEN**, LOVESWEPT #325, by Mary Kay McComas, a breathtaking angel drives Joe Bonner off the road, calls him a trespasser, then faints dead away in his arms. Leslie Rothe had run away from her sister's wedding in confusion, wondering if she'd ever fall

(continued)

in love—or if she even wanted to. Joe awakened turbulent emotions, teased her unmercifully, then kissed her breathless, and taught a worldly woman with an innocent heart how it felt to love a man. But could she prove how much she treasured Joe before her folly destroyed their love?

Next, we introduce an incredibly wonderful treat to you. Deborah Smith begins her Cherokee Trilogy with **SUNDANCE AND THE PRINCESS**, LOVESWEPT #325. (The second romance in the trilogy, **TEMPTING THE WOLF**, will be on sale in June; the final love story, **KAT'S TALE**, will be on sale in August.) In **SUNDANCE AND THE PRINCESS** Jeopard Surprise is Robert Redford gorgeous, a golden-haired outlaw whose enigmatic elegance enthralls Tess Gallatin, makes her want to break all the rules—and lose herself in his arms! He'd come aboard her boat pretending to court the blue-eyed Cherokee princess, but his true mission—to search for a stolen diamond—was endangered by Tess's sweet, seductive laugh. Tess could deny Jep nothing, not her deepest secrets or her mother's precious remembrance, but she never suspected her lover might betray her . . . or imagined how fierce his fury might blaze. An incandescent love story, not to be missed.

LOST IN THE WILD, LOVESWEPT #327, by Gail Douglas, features impossibly gorgeous Nick Corcoran, whose mesmerizing eyes make Tracy Carlisle shiver with desire. But her shyness around her grandfather's corporate heir apparent infuriates her! For three years Nick had considered her off limits, and besides, he had no intention of romancing the snobbish granddaughter of his powerful boss to win the top job. But when Tracy outsmarted a pair of kidnappers and led him into the forest in a desperate escape plan, Nick was enchanted by this courageous woodswoman who embraced danger and risked her life to save his. But could Tracy persuade Nick that by choice she wasn't his rival, only his prize?

(continued)

Peggy Webb gives us pure dynamite in **ANY THURS-DAY,** LOVESWEPT #328. Hannah Donovan is a sexy wildcat of a woman, Jim Roman decided as she pointed her rifle at his chest—definitely a quarry worthy of his hunt! With a devilish, devastating smile, the rugged columnist began his conquest of this beautiful Annie Oakley by kissing her with expert, knowing lips . . . and Hannah felt wicked, wanton passion brand her cool scientist's heart. Jim wore power and danger like a cloak, challenged and intrigued her as few men ever had—but she had to show him she couldn't be tamed . . . or possessed. Could they stop fighting destiny and each other long enough to bridge their separate worlds? A fabulous romance!

Remember Dr. Delilah Jones? In **WAITING FOR LILA,** LOVESWEPT #329, Billie Green returns to her characters of old for a raucous good time. Lila had special plans for the medical conference in Acapulco—this trip she was determined to bag a husband! She enlisted her best friends as matchmakers, invited them to produce the perfect candidate—rich, handsome, successful—then spotted the irresistibly virile man of her dreams all by herself. Bill Shelley was moonstruck by the elegant lady with the voice like raw silk, captivated by this mysterious, seductive angel who seemed to have been made just for him. Once he knew her secrets, could Bill convince her that nothing would keep her as safe and happy as his enduring love? A pure delight from Billie!

Enjoy!

Carolyn Nichols

Carolyn Nichols
Editor
LOVESWEPT
Bantam Books
666 Fifth Avenue
New York, NY 10103